Child of the Devil

by No Fenne

Lucifer, Terror Knight

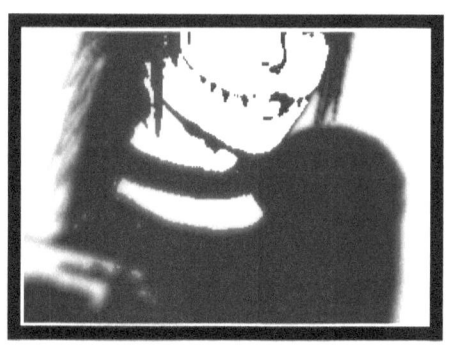

"Luna's uncanny countenance."

TABLE OF CONTENTS

THE HOLY AXUDO

———

"Send my child to the overworld. He shall perish; lest the prophecy ring true."

— Terra 13:9

"It is done, Lord. He lays by the lair of a She-Devil. I have no doubts His brief life will soon come to a pass."

— Terra 13:25

PROLOGUE

On planet Earth, many believe there to be two gods. One, the father of creation, benevolence, and forgiveness. They refer to him as God. He who created mankind; their ideals, their futures, their fates. He who resides in heaven, a place those worthy enough will join.

His counterpart is known as the Devil. He who destroys, begets suffering—the opposite of the heavenly father. Those who wronged in their natural life would suffer for eternity in hell upon their death. The Devil, as it were, could not be considered completely evil—for it was he who dealt punishment to the deserved.

What many believe, however, is not necessarily the truth. In fact, for mortals in general, there is no way for them to know whether or not gods, or a god, even exists at all. Perhaps it was luck, perhaps there was an intuition given to them by birth, that they figured out about the two gods. And for millennia, they worshipped their sacred god. The majority, the Heavenly Father; a select few, the Devil.

In truth, there was a god. But only one. One who both creates and destroys. He who gave life, He who takes it away. Unfortunately, or maybe fortunately, depending on who would view it, this god was far more like the Devil that mortals spoke of than the heavenly Father.

His name is Satan. In the underworld he resides, watching over Earth. Or, more accurately, not watching at all. He had given life to the planet and sat and watched for some time. He even created the first humans in his likeness to see what would happen, to watch their little lives, see what they'd do. But after a while, it got tiring, and he stopped paying attention. He would tend to himself instead, pleasuring himself with the torture of the dead who'd entered his realm.

He had a lovely wife, Lumia, but they could never have a child. For he knew as the prophecy foretold:

> *The child of the devil,*
> *Languishes at his peril.*
> *He who shall seek retribution,*
> *On the father of creation.*

— ??????

CHAPTER 1

An unwanted child

Lucia knew she couldn't keep the act forever. At some point, Satan would get suspicious of her being sick for this long. But all she could do was hope and pray, for she could not stop the child in her belly from growing; the child of Satan.

She'd first noticed her belly growing several months ago. At first, she thought she was getting a bit fat. She knew how Satan was, the indignant fury he'd have if she were to have gotten any heavier. She had immediately cut down on her intake and tried to starve herself, but the belly kept growing regardless. Some time later, there it was—the soft sound of a heartbeat. At first, it was a faint pulse from within her, one that was indistinguishable from her own. But one lonely night, after a session with Satan, as she lay on her bed alone in her thoughts and scared of her unusual weight gain, she heard it clearly.

>*Thump...*
>
>*Thump...*
>
>*Thump...*

Lucia knew then she was pregnant. At first, she was relieved. She hadn't become fat, and as such, she would not be punished for that reason. But her feelings soon gave way to intense fear: *the prophecy*.

Everyone knew about the prophecy; the rule for Satan to never have a child. But, as a god, Satan was never supposed to be able to conceive a child. He created himself that way, after all. As such, Lucia had never expected this to happen. What changed this time around? Whatever the case, she knew that if Satan found out, she and her child would both be killed. She had to think of a plan—and fast. If her belly grew any larger, Satan would definitely notice.

It came to her in the following days; she'd pretend to be severely ill. That way, she could stay out of sight, as Satan did not want to linger around his wives if they were sick. A foolproof plan in the short term—but how long could she do it before Satan got suspicious?

—

"Lady Lucia! Your breakfast is ready!" yelled out a maid. Lucia sat on her bed, still feigning illness. A few of the maids knew of her predicament and did their best to keep Satan away from her as much as possible. Noticing her maid, Lucia welcomed her in.

"Come in, Paisy."

The maid opened the door and rolled the breakfast tray in. The old metal tray sat on top of a flimsy trolley, which made a creaking noise as it rattled along the wooden bedroom floor. On the tray itself was the usual gruel and porridge combo, made specially for the sick lady.

"Ew, this again, Paisy?" said Lucia, cracking a grin. She already knew she'd get this. Satan wanted her *active* as soon as possible, so she had to eat 'healthy' foods, as he called it. It'd been quite some time by now, and even *he* had something in him that was worried.

"Ah, of course! I made your favourite, my lady," sparked up Paisy. "I even added some porridge in the gruel as you so desire."

The bulge on Lucia's stomach was quite evident at this point. The baby was surely due any time now; Lucia just had to hold out a bit longer. *Just a bit longer, my dear child, and you will survive the first step in your life. It'll only get harder after that...*

Paisy carefully brought the tray over to Lucia and over the bump. Lucia, still rubbing her belly softly, looked up at Paisy and spoke quietly.

"Isn't it beautiful? That even in the land of the dead, life can still be created."

Paisy nodded. She couldn't speak her mind, as she knew—as did everyone else—that the baby would not live long in this world; not with Satan around.

—

Lucia was now huddled in the kitchen pantry, clutching the month-old babe in her arms. In the dead of night, Satan had come in, apparently unsatisfied with his other wives, Melanie and Risa. He desired—no, craved, Lucia. He hadn't slept with her in months; he didn't care if she was sick, she'd have to do.

What he found enraged him, however. Lucia wasn't sick at all; in fact, she was bearing his child the entire time. She'd lay there, cradling the baby and singing softly, when he came in.

The moment he entered, she stared at him, the fear evident in her eyes. She knew she was done.

They stared at each other for what seemed like an eternity before Satan slowly backed away, a grin on his face. Lucia knew what that meant—he was going to punish her, probably to her death.

She ran out of her room and tried to find a way to escape the castle, but guards were at every exit, blocking them, following a lockdown order. They immediately understood the situation when they saw the child. The fourth wife of Satan was soon to be killed, and it wouldn't be a sight any of them wanted to see.

–

"My lady, this way!" spoke a hushed voice. Lucia turned around, startled. She was in the middle of the castle hallway with nowhere to go. Guards blocked every exit, and the castle's interior furniture was sparse, lending her nowhere to hide. She'd almost given up until she heard her maid. There was Paisy, holding open the now unlocked kitchen door with her left hand, and beckoning for Lucia with her right.

"Quick, before he comes!" yelled Paisy to Lucia.

Lucia rushed into the kitchen. It was dimly lit, making it difficult to see. The few candles that were lit were a smoky yellow, flickering every now and then, casting shadows on the central table which was bolted to the floor. Because it was night, the kitchen was mostly empty. A few dishes were left out to dry, and some barrels here and there. It didn't seem like there was much to hide behind. But anything was better than standing in the middle of the hallway. She'd have to make do with whatever Paisy had planned.

As it was quite dark, she had to slow down. She took each step carefully, making sure not to lose grip on her child, avoiding a risky fall. Behind her, Paisy closed the kitchen door and put on both locks. It wouldn't stop Satan, but might slow him down, or even make him think no one was there.

The kitchen had no other exit, however. If Satan did manage to figure out Lucia was in there, there would be no escape. Lucia would have to hide; scanning the area, however, caused Lucia to realize that she didn't see any place that could fit her and her child. Lucia looked to Paisy, fearful. Paisy looked back, the reassuring gaze evident she had something up her sleeve.

"He might not look in the pantry. Look, it's hidden. Hide here, my lady." Paisy had opened a small door near the back of the kitchen. It was slightly hidden behind a scrawny wine barrel. It was a small storage room, not exactly made for people, but there was just enough room to fit a woman and her child. This could definitely work—Satan would-n't be able to see Lucia from the outside.

Lucia pushed in the baby first, then entered after. The baby was awake, but did not cry. *Stay strong, my dear Lucifer.*

Before closing the pantry door, Lucia

looked up at Paisy's face. Paisy had a grim smile on, even when faced with this terrible situation. "Paisy, you are so brave. Thank you," said Lucia.

Paisy closed the pantry door from the out-side, leaving Lucia and Lucifer in the dark, lit up only by light coming from a small crack in the door. Her child stared up at her, his innocent face not recognizing the peril they were in. She gave him a smile, then clutched him towards her bosom. She wouldn't let go of him, no matter what. Satan would have to kill her to get to him.

Lucia could hear her own heartbeats as the moments passed by. She could hear her own breath, her child's breathing. Silence. A breath here and there. The thump of her child's heart resounding in her chest. It seemed like an eternity had passed, yet nothing happened. Perhaps Satan didn't want to kill her? Could she have read his expression wrong? He'd always been an easy read, though. Maybe it was due to the time she hadn't seen him; he could've changed slightly after a few months of not seeing her. *But no,* she thought. *He's more likely playing a sick game with me.*

Suddenly, there was a loud crash from outside. The kitchen door, made of hard timber and braced with metal joints, cracked and split in two as Satan sliced it open with ease with his cleaver sword.

Splinters shot out and nails flew across the kitchen as he retracted his sword from the now-broken door. In the kitchen, Paisy screamed, panicking. She hadn't expected him to barge in like that.

"The guards spotted you letting Lucia in here, slave. Where is she?" snivelled Satan. Paisy, shaking but still putting on a brave face, seemed unnerved as she gave her answer.

"I do not know what you are talking about, my Lord."

She kept her head down and looked at the ground, careful not to look Satan in the eyes. If she'd looked, she would have seen that Satan had a grin on his face. Satan already knew the answer, but was testing out the maid's loyalty. *It looks like she's loyal to Lucia, not me,* thought Satan. *Wrong choice, slave.*

"Well, I know five guards are definitely more trustworthy than one maid… especially a maid who happens to always serve Lucia."

Paisy froze in place. The guards had ratted her out, and now there was no denying it. But Lucia was her lady—she would not give her up, no matter the cost.

"I do not know what you are talking about, my Lor—"

Paisy's head flew off her body before she could finish her sentence. Her head landed on the floor with a dull *thud.* Once there, it rolled around briefly, before coming to a stop. Blood poured from her head, along with other contents that once belonged inside her skull. Her body crumpled to the floor, lifeless. More blood spewed out of her neck hole and onto the floor, staining it an ugly red.

Satan's blade, which usually was a glistening gold, was now dripping with fresh blood, turning his blade a shiny golden-red. Satan held his blade up, turning and twisting it, admiring its beauty. It was that much more beautiful with blood on it, and it desired more. And more it shall have.

"Lucia, my dear, come out. I just want to talk, that's all."

Satan spoke softly, unlike himself. It felt calm… soothing. *Could he have changed?* From inside the pantry, Lucia hesitated. *No, he was Satan. The Devil. He was always evil, and always will be. Why would he change now, especially now that his own life was in jeopardy?*

Lucia remained quiet. She was hidden quite well, and Satan never went into the kitchen. The kitchen was for the cooks and maids, after all. She doubt he knew about the pantry, when Lucia herself (who used to cook sometimes before she got pregnant) didn't know about it at all. Maybe he wouldn't be able to find her, maybe… but then again, he was God, so anything could be possible.

"Ah, smart little slave. She even covered this door with a measly wine barrel. Too bad I'm much smarter than any of you," sneered Satan as he pushed the heavy barrel aside. Behind it was a small door, but definitely large enough to fit a person through. The door was simple and made out of wood. The handle was made of iron, but had long seen better days. It was rusted now, and almost falling off.

"Let's see what treasures we find in here —," said Satan as he grasped the handle and pulled. Inside the pantry sat Lucia and her month-old child. Lucia stared at him, her mouth agape, terrified. Satan snickered as he reached in.

"Ah! We find my dear Lucia in here! Come out now." Satan dragged Lucia and the baby out.

Remarkably, the baby remained silent throughout this endeavour, his face unchanging throughout the events of the night.

"Satan, please, dear… oh please…" sobbed Lucia. Only now did she see Paisy's headless body. The maid's blood was smeared across the kitchen floor, leaving a horrifying red glare reflecting from the dim candles that laced the kitchen. It was a horrific sight to see, one that no one should ever witness. Her child looked down and stared. His face remained stoic, likely not comprehending what was in front of him.

"You tried to hide this from me, but you should've known better. I created this world. I created *you*. I know everything, Lucia. You are foolish to think otherwise."

Satan dragged Lucia up by the neck, partially choking her in the process. Lucia couldn't speak; all she could think of was to try to breathe. *I must survive; if not for anything else, for my child.*

"Unfortunate as it is, I don't think I can kill this child that easily here. I'll have Grim send him to the overworld to die. You, on the other hand, are no more."

With that said, Satan ran his bloody sword through Lucia. The giant sword pierced her chest, then her lungs, then finished its journey once outside of her back. Satan grabbed the child from Lucia and then pulled his blade out of Lucia's body. Her body fell down—hard. A large pool of blood formed underneath her, which soon mixed with her fallen maid's. As Satan walked away, the kitchen floor seemed to flood with the red liquid. It turned the whole floor a reddish brown, something that would take more than a day to clean.

–

It is here where one story ends—and another begins.

CHAPTER 2

Lost in the forest of evil

"Sir, is that… is that the sound of a crying babe?" Sergeant Johnny Mackintosh stopped his horse and peered around. They were on a remote path close to the dangerous forest of evil, yet somehow he could hear a baby's cry. Not hearing an answer, he called out to his squadron members again. "Does anyone else hear this?"

"You've keen ears, Mack. But yes, I hear it faintly."

General Lenkl Deniere had helped lead his army to victory a week ago. After years of war, the kingdom of Terre finally got rid of the uprising forces of the Devil's Cult. Devilish spawn, they were. They worshipped the Devil and had planned on overthrowing King Bastea. As the king's top general, Deniere had been called away from his home in Northern Terre and sent to fight when it started. He'd sorely missed his life in Northern Terre, which, while snowy and cold, was peaceful and happy. As soon as the war ended, he immediately left Middle Terre to return home.

The squadron spread out, looking for what could be making the sound. It surely couldn't be a child, not this close to the forest of evil. The forest of evil had a shortcut, one that Deniere used to get home faster. It was risky, though, as the forest had a dangerous reputation, hence its name. Those who ventured deep never returned. There were myths, rumours, legends—whatever you wanted to call it, there was talk of a monster who lived there. The fabled 'succubus', a beautiful lady who would charm men with her beauty, then kill and *eat* them. A wild tale, sure, but as people went missing over the years, it was one that never strayed too far out of the realm of possibility. As such, Deniere never ventured too far in. Luckily, the shortcut path was near the clearing, so it was safe—well, safe enough for him.

As a skilled and experienced fighter, Deniere was confident in his own ability. As long as he stayed near the edge of the forest, he wasn't worried. He was also surrounded by his contingent of experienced soldiers; they were battle-hardened men who served in the war. They weren't afraid of anything; a single monster, who might not even exist, surely didn't frighten them.

"Everyone, look! It really is a baby!" shouted out Mackintosh. The sergeant had wandered slightly off the path, a bit deeper into the forest, and was now holding up a child. Apparently, he had found it crying on the forest floor, completely alone, with only a crude diaper on.

Deniere rushed over. Sure enough, Mackintosh held a baby in his arms. Mackintosh, unsure of what to do next, questioned his leader. "Uh… what do we do with it?"

Deniere gently took it in his arms. He and his wife were never able to have a child, as his wife was infertile. He knew that she wanted one, that she felt sad she couldn't give him an heir. Perhaps this was the grace of God? Or a message to Deniere? *I have no heir. Perhaps I could raise this one as my own?*

The child stopped crying and stared at him. Deniere looked down at its innocent face, smiling. *He kind of looks like me too,* thought Deniere. *Mary will definitely be pleased.*

—

"It's practice time, Lucifer!" shouted out Deniere. Lucifer groaned in anguish. Sword practice always hurt, as his father never took it easy on him. He slid his blanket over his head and hoped that the calls would fade away.

"LUCIFER! I know you can hear me!" yelled out Deniere. "Out. NOW!"

Lucifer let out a heavy sigh, then finally got out of bed. It was always the days he was most tired that practice would occur. Then again, practice was every day, so he was tired every day.

—

The swords clanged as father and son struck and parried each other's slashes. Already an expert, Lucifer was matching his father in speed and technique. All he was lacking now was strength; something he'd get as he grew older. Even as young as he was, Deniere didn't take it easy on him, to make sure Lucifer was as skilled as one possibly could be.

Deniere swung an overhand strike, fast too. Lucifer dodged it and countered with a horizontal slash. Deniere blocked it with his own sword, then hopped back.

"Getting stronger, son. Remarkably so!"

Lucifer swung again, expecting his father to

block. His father did, and so he followed up with a quick stab towards him. His father tried to parry the attack, but wasn't quite fast enough. Lucifer's sword slightly pierced his father's chest armour before he stopped himself. Surprised, Lucifer retracted his blade and took a step back.

"Father, you didn't say stop…?"

Lucifer was confused. Did his father think they stopped sparring? He would usually tell him to stop when they did so, otherwise they were supposed to keep sparring.

His father clutched his wound, looking for blood. There was a little, but luckily the armour had blocked most of the energy. He turned his hand around, examining the blood that did come out. It wasn't too bad, just a small scrape. Raising his head, he spoke.

"No, Lucifer—you're just faster than me now." Deniere panted heavily, as he was out of breath. "You even almost took out your old man there." His son wasn't even a teen yet, and he was already faster and stronger than him. The kid was something unnatural—not that it mattered, anyhow. He was all a parent could ever ask for. Lucifer was a good kid; smart, strong, kind, and treated others well. He almost seemed *too perfect.*

Deniere had promised Lucifer that he'd take him out hunting in the forest when he was old enough to beat him in a spar. However, Deniere had thought that Lucifer would be an adult at that time, not still a kid. The nearest hunting ground was in the forest of evil, after all. It was an enigmatic place that not even Deniere liked to visit. A bounty hunter had recently disappeared there, too. Probably unrelated to anything concerning the 'monster' rumour, but one could never be certain.

Deniere didn't really believe in those rumours, but even so, never ventured too far. He couldn't risk that when he had a territory and people to take care of, after all; besides, there wasn't really any reason to go too deep in the forest, anyway, aside from the *monster*.

Lucifer, on the other hand, was always intrigued by the stories of the forest and wanted to venture deep inside. As such, it was what drove him to spar even when he didn't want to—because he knew one day he'd win and get his chance.

—

It was just the two of them on the hunting trip. Lucifer had invited his mother, Mary, to join as well, but she refused, not being a stickler for hunting; also, it was a cold winter, and she didn't like going out in the icy snow. It was quite the harsh winter this year around, and one could freeze to death if one were to be caught in a blizzard. The sky didn't foreshadow good weather either; even so, Lucifer insisted they go, not wanting to waste any time. He earned the reward, after all, so Deniere had to oblige.

Deniere had packed only his own hunting bow and a set of arrows. His son wasn't allowed to have any hunting weapons, as he was still too young. As expected, Lucifer was in a grumpy mood. He thought that he would be able to do the hunting on the trip; but no, he would only be there to see what happened. His excitement had turned into disappointment, then into boredom as they slowly traversed through the snowy forest.

They had travelled some distance into the forest before Deniere readied up his bow. Here was the prime area for hunting deer. Not too close to the edge, not too deep in the forest. A good middle ground, and a common place for deer to frolic.

"Do you see any deer? If you see one, don't shout. They can hear very well," lectured Deniere. Lucifer seemed to perk up upon hearing that, and looked around as well. This would be his first hunt, and in the *forest of evil* no less. Even if he wasn't hunting, this was still mildly exciting.

"Shh!" Deniere held his bow taught, his gaze fixed onto a deer in the distance. The deer was old and seemed to have worse hearing than normal. It was grazing on a snow-covered plant, unknowingly in the sights of a seasoned hunter. It appeared to have a limping leg as well, perhaps injured while escaping a predator. *Its time has come,* thought Lenkl Deniere. *If not by me, then by a wolf. Forgive me for this hunt, dear deer.*

Lucifer, however, wasn't paying attention anymore. He had spotted a rabbit and decided to follow it. He had already forgotten about the deer hunt; his mind was now buzzing with questions relating to the small rodent in front of him. Did rabbits live in holes? In trees? There was one way to find out—by following it to its home. The best way to learn was to observe it in nature, after all.

—

The deer slumped to the snow floor, dead. Deniere's arrow struck its heart, killing it quickly. A clean kill, but not unusual for the expert bowman. Deniere stood up and prepared to walk over.

"Did you see what I did, Lucifer? I hit it in the heart, so it died quickly—hopefully without pain. Lucifer?" Deniere looked around, not hearing a response. To his dismay, his son wasn't there. He was just there a moment ago—he couldn't have gone far, could he?

Deniere cupped his hands together and shouted. "Lucifer? Lucifer! Where did you go?"

–

The rabbit ran underneath a bush, shaking some snow off its leaves. *So that's where they live!* thought Lucifer. He quickly looked under the bush, but there was no rabbit in sight. Hearing a rustle from further ahead, he quickly poked his head up and saw some snow in the distance move. Apparently, the rabbit had only passed by the bush—and was now long gone.

Lucifer sighed. *I guess I'll just learn the boring way... I'll just ask someone.* Learning from the library was boring, and often difficult at times.

He wasn't the best at learning through words, he needed to see stuff to learn. Books with pictures did help, but they were expensive and quite rare.

Amidst his thoughts, he snapped back to reality. Looking around, all he saw were snow-covered trees, none of which he recognized. The sun reflected off the snow on the forest floor harshly, making the landscape appear the same in every direction. A blizzard had started to pick up some time ago which caused snow to fill in his tracks, so he couldn't retrace his steps. Where exactly was he? He wasn't… lost in the forest, was he?

The blizzard picked up quickly. Lucifer was still in his normal clothes, not prepared for a snowstorm. He didn't want bulky clothes on in case they made too much noise during the hunt, but now he regretted that decision. *It's so cold. I have to find father soon.*

He slowly wandered through the cold forest, unsure of what direction he was heading towards, but hoping that by going in a straight line, he'd eventually make it out of the forest. Everywhere he walked, however, was just trees and snow, and it was getting colder and darker by the minute. Soon, he'd have to rest; he needed to find a building, a house; something with a roof and walls, as he knew he'd probably freeze in the open. At this point, he'd need to find *anything.*

I can't die here… father, where are you?

Lucifer now struggled to raise his legs against the rising snow. The falling snow and dropping temperatures had only gotten worse as the night progressed. It was difficult to see where he was going, what with the snow and darkness obscuring his vision. Surely the castle guards were out looking for him by now? Then again, maybe not. It was too dangerous to search right now—but if so, they might think he was already dead. *I know father will keep searching for me, no matter what... at least, I hope so.* Was it selfish of him to want his father to save him? To put his own life at risk for a search? Maybe it was, but—

BONK.

His head collided with a rock wall. Lucifer stumbled back, dizzy, and looked in front of him. There stood a large rock wall... or door, more likely. It had budged a bit and an outline was visible which separated a section of the wall from the rest. He slowly turned his head around, grasping the view of the building in front of him. It looked like an abandoned stone fort of sorts; it was old, falling apart, and some parts were caved in. In any case, he had no other option—he was freezing to death. He'd have to go inside. He shoved the door with all his might, and it budged a little more. *Just a bit more...* He was almost out of strength—it was now or never. He shoved it two more times before it finally opened.

The inside of the stone building was very dark, but at least it was free of snow. Right behind the door were three stairsteps that led down to a pathway of sorts. No time to look, though—Lucifer closed the heavy stone door behind him to stop the freezing wind from piercing the inside air.

It was surprisingly warm inside the stone building, indicating the presence of an active heating source; fire. *There has to be a fireplace close by… maybe someone lives here.*

To the left, the passageway ended abruptly. The wall had caved in there long ago, leaving nothing more than a stack of stone rubble. To the right was a long hallway which seemed decently intact, however. There was a small candle dimly lit at the end, giving off a small yellow glow in the otherwise dark place. Adjacent to the candle was a slight opening with light pouring through. It had to be a door; behind it were definitely signs of life—a bright light source, for one.

As the blizzard continued to howl outside, Lucifer slowly walked down the hallway. His gaze focused on the candle; it became closer and closer as he trotted towards it, until he came upon it, almost burning himself—his head still aching from the cold. There was a feeling of warmth coming from the left side; the door. It was left slightly ajar, so some heat and light came out of it, adding to the warmth at the end of the hallway.

Peering through it, Lucifer could make out parts of the room behind the door. It was a large, squarish expanse, with a cauldron in the middle. The cauldron had a large fire blazing; its thick smoke billowing up into the ceiling of the place. *That must be the source of heat.* For the flame to be alive in the cold, someone must have been tending to it.

Lucifer opened the door and walked inside. The heat of the cauldron instantly comforted his cold skin. Looking around, there were candles placed on the walls of the room, evenly spaced apart. And from the roof, hung—

Lucifer stopped in his tracks, eyes wide in

horror.

There were three human skeletons hanging from the ceiling. Lucifer had never seen a skeleton before, so this was very frightening to the almost teen. He'd heard of his dad's stories; the gruesome things General Deniere had to do and saw in the war. But to experience it firsthand, especially as a kid, was something Lucifer was not prepared for.

Who... who did this? Lucifer's mind raced. *The forest of evil... the rumours are true!* It seemed that indeed, there was a monster who lived deep in the forest... and unwittingly, Lucifer had stumbled right into its lair.

–

"Why—why are you here?" Her voice startled Lucifer. The voice, highish pitch and raspy, came from behind the cauldron.

Lucifer stepped to the side and peered through the flames; it was then he saw who spoke.

She was a slim, young lady, only a few

years older than him. Her hair was long and dark, glowing slightly red from the hue of the flames, and tied up into a long ponytail that flowed down her spine. Covering her mouth and nose was a bandana-mask thing, made of a black cloth. She wore dark shoulder pauldrons; a black shirt underneath, torn from the chest down, revealing her athletic torso; her black leggings were tight fitting, but had seen better days; with a short, homemade cape tied to her waist.

What was most striking wasn't her longs-word that she had drawn, which was pointed at Lucifer; it was her face. Even with part of it covered, Lucifer could see that she was beautiful—too beautiful, in fact. She didn't seem *human* some-how. But the longsword that was drawn was also important, and probably should have been more at the forefront of his thoughts.

"Uh..." Lucifer struggled for words. Then all of a sudden, it seemed as if he lost all his strength. The cold temperatures and his long journey through the thick snow had taken its toll.

As he fell to the ground, he could see the girl rush towards him. Who was she, and why did she live here? *Why are there skeletons hanging on the roof?* Lucifer's questions drifted away as he soon became unconscious.

–

The cauldron fire's warm crackle woke him up. It was a low, grumbling sound, but soothing to hear; the same sound he'd heard from the fireplace at Castle Gruppen many times on winter nights, with his mother reading him a book to sleep. It was comforting, soothing; almost tricking him into thinking he was back at home.

Lucifer slowly opened his eyes and peered around. He lay on the stone ground on a raggedy blanket. The rag had no smell and looked quite ancient. *Maybe from the time this building was built.* He turned his head towards the fire, where he could hear someone humming. It was the girl; her slender figure cast a light shadow over him as she cooked something over the fire.

> *"In a land very far away,*
> *The devil beckons us to stay.*
> *Cast aside, the downtrodden few,*
> *Against odds, enter heaven's queue.*
> *And others, neutral as they are;*
> *Can be forgiven, through and through.*
> *For evil men who dare for more,*
> *The gates of hell opens its door."*

It was a nice, soothing tune, but the lyrics did not seem to match the beautiful melody. The words somehow felt sinister… if songs could somehow be so. Lucifer's stomach then rumbled. The smell of the cooked food had woken up his body, and it wanted nourishment now, as he hadn't had a meal in a while.

The girl, hearing the complaint, turned around. She saw that Lucifer was staring at her.

Lucifer then noticed her eyes; they were a sharp and piercing green, an eye colour he'd never seen before. He'd only ever seen two; black and blue were all he'd seen growing up in Gruppen. He did hear of green, or hazel eyes, but supposedly, it was quite rare in Terre.

"You're hungry, human. Don't just stare, come over here." The girl patted the floor space beside her, motioning for him to come sit down beside her. Lucifer nervously came over, unsure of her intentions; her longsword, while sheathed, was still within her reach.

Unaware of Lucifer's fears, she scooped up the cooked broth into a small bowl and handed it to him in a quick motion. It smelled of a mixture of meat and vegetables, something simple but nice at the same time.

—

Over the course of the meal, Lucifer explained his story to the girl. The hunt, the forest rumours, the blizzard; and finally, finding the stone building. She kept silent the whole time, listening to the story intently. Only when he finished did she speak.

"So you weren't here to kill me...?" she questioned. Her brow was raised, still unsure of him. Humans, after all, were always bad. They were *monsters* who killed without remorse, beings who thought of no one other than themselves. But this one was still a child; he didn't even hold a weapon. He seemed different, not at all evil. His story made some sense too; he wasn't looking for her in particular, he was just trying to survive.

"No ma'am... what do you mean? Why would I want to kill you?" Lucifer was incredulous at this statement. That was a bit extreme, was it not? In what world would he try to kill a random person? In his mind, it made no sense.

The girl spoke, breaking up his scattered thoughts. "Nevermind, human. You're different from the others I've met," she said. She studied his face before continuing. "My name is Luna. What is yours?"

Lucifer cleared his throat before replying. He didn't want to sound scared in front of her, after all.

"I'm Lucifer… Lucifer Deniere…"

Lucifer froze. What would he say next? He panicked, unsure of what to say. All of a sudden he couldn't speak. It was like his mind suddenly went blank; something Lucifer hadn't experienced before. Lucifer and Luna stared at each other awkwardly for a moment, before Lucifer continued.

"Is your name just Luna? What about your last name?" finished Lucifer. Everyone he knew had a last name; a good save by him. The family name that was passed on from generation to generation. Maybe he'd know of her relatives in Gruppen, if she had any.

"I don't have a last name. I have always just been Luna," she replied. Her face looked kind of sad when she said that. Lucifer noticed, but said nothing, unsure what to make of it. "Anyway, *Luc*, when you're done with your soup, put the bowl over there," Luna motioned to a small table by the west wall, "and stick close to the fire, because I don't have any more blankets. Okay?"

Lucifer nodded. This place was scary, but the lady was nice. Some things still unnerved him, however. *Why do people want to kill her? Were those skeletons people who tried to kill her? Probably...* Those questions could be answered another time. What mattered now was that he was warm and safe; that is to say, at least, for the time being.

–

"Wake up, Luc," Luna shook Lucifer gently. "The blizzard's over for now; it's afternoon. The perfect time for you to get home safe."

Lucifer groggily sat up to get his bearings. Through a small gap near the roof, on the east wall, he could just barely see the outside world. Sunlight shone through the gap, illuminating the room a tad.

Luna held out her hand to Lucifer, and he held on. Her hand was soft and delicate. *These were not the hands of a labourer, but one of a noble,* thought Lucifer. She lifted him up and led him towards the southern part of the room, which housed the entrance and exit to the ancient stone building.

She spoke to Lucifer in a hushed voice. "Lucky for you, Luc, I know this forest very well. I'll get you home in no time, don't you worry."

Lucifer thought he could see a big grin from underneath her mask. *Why does she wear a mask? I'd like to see the rest of her face,* he thought. *She's so pretty.*

–

The snow was quite deep; Lucifer, being quite short since he was still only twelve, struggled to wade through the heavy snow. At some points, Luna even had to pick him up and carry him over very deep sections. It was a long and tiring walk; but before evening, they reached the forest's end. There lay the forest shortcut, leading to the town of Gruppen, where the Denieres ruled.

Lucifer took a few steps forward, away from the forest, then stopped. He turned around; Luna was there, watching him.

Noticing his abrupt stop, Luna realized what Lucifer expected.

"I can't leave the forest, Luc. Humans don't seem to like me, after all."

The expression of a pained smile was visible in her eyes. Lucifer barely understood it at the time, but knew that she wasn't exactly human. She was the evil in the forest, the *monster* everyone spoke of, but even so, she was kind. She didn't seem evil. *She wasn't evil*. Lucifer ran back to her and gave her a hug.

"Thank you, Luna."

Luna was surprised by this. No one had ever shown her this kindness before, but it was a good feeling, a happy one. A warm feeling she had never experienced before. They stood still, holding each other for a moment. Then, she spoke.

"The sun will set soon, Luc. Your family must be worried about you."

With a parting wave, Lucifer set off for Gruppen.

Underneath her mask, Luna had a smile. She'd probably never see this human again, but it made her happy to know that not all humans were bad... at least as long as they didn't know that she was a succubus. As she trotted back to her home in the forest, she wondered: would he have been so kind to her if she wasn't wearing her mask, if he'd seen her razor-sharp teeth...?

CHAPTER 3

A fateful war beckons

Sergeant Mackintosh rushed into the throne room of Castle Gruppen, out of breath. He'd been sprinting to get there as quickly as possible as soon as he received the bad news from the messenger. General Deniere sat on the throne, in the middle of talking to his wife, Mary. Deniere looked at Mackintosh, who looked a mess. He waited for the Sergeant, who took a moment to compose himself. When he did, he spoke hurriedly.

"My lord, King Bastea requests your assistance—immediately."

Surprised by this, General Deniere responded quickly. "Surely the Devil cult hasn't resurrected itself? Or is it of another matter?"

Mack shook his head. "I'm not entirely sure. Some self-proclaimed 'dictator-king', a 'King' Ranken, has gathered quite a large army. He claims that 'might makes right', and will prove that to King Bastea soon."

General Deniere hung his head in disapproval, but knew what he had to do. Duty called; once again, he would have to leave his family and go out to war. He looked at Mary, who smiled back at him, understanding. *I'm sorry, my dear, but I must leave for the battlefield once more.*

–

Lucifer was woken up late at night. He was tired, but this seemed important. His father led him down the stairs to the room he was never allowed in. It was located deep in the basement of the castle, and you had to traverse a maze of sections and corridors to get to it. No candles or lights were lit in this area of the castle, so his father brought with him a portable lantern to illuminate the area.

The specific room in question was behind a locked door, one made of brilliant gold and laced with diamonds. It was inordinately heavy; he'd tried to open it before, but wasn't able to. His parents had never told him what was behind the door, but he never did ask.   In fact, he never told them that he'd seen it before. He assumed it was supposed to be a secret due to the fact of its hidden nature, and the fact that no one had bothered to tell him about it.

His father pushed the door open slowly, grunting in exertion. It was clearly difficult, but soon, he managed. The gold door swung inwards; it made no noise, as if the grease on its hinges were still fresh. Once the door opened, Lucifer peered inside the room. It was a small, generic-looking room. A thin veil of dust covered the wooden floor; it was evident that this room had not been touched in many years.

At the end of the room was a table, and

beside it, a full suit of unusual-looking armour. On the table, encased in a dull glass case, was a long and slightly curved dark-silver sword. The case and table were attached together with what seemed like a locking mechanism; confirming that was the presence of a three-pin rotary lock, located in the front face of the table.

His father placed his hand on the case lightly, inspecting the sword inside. Then, he turned to face Lucifer.

"My son, this sword is yours…" He walked over to the suit of armour, looking at it up and down. Then, he continued. "On your twentieth birthday, you may open the case. When that time comes, you shall know how to open it."

Lucifer was confused. The sword was huge, and the armour scary looking. But that wasn't what troubled him. How would he magically know how to open the case by then? Was he supposed to guess the numbers? And why did he have to open it?

When you don't know, you ask, thought Lucifer. *Well, at least that's what father always tells me.*

Finishing his thoughts, Lucifer spoke up. "Father, why can't you open it? Didn't you put the sword in there to begin with?"

Deniere sighed softly. His son was still young, too young perhaps, to understand the gravity of the situation.

"Yes, I did. But I will have to go to fight for King Bastea soon. There is a chance I may not be returning home. In that case, you will have to open this case yourself."

"But you will come home, right dad? You always do."

Lucifer looked at his dad, his eyes gleaming with confidence. His dad was always so strong and brave. He'd heard of his war stories of before he was born, his exploits against the Devil's cult. If nothing else, he was sure his dad would come home —that he was sure of.

"Of course I will, Lucifer. I promised your mother that, and I don't intend on breaking that promise." Deniere had a smile on his face. He never did break a promise, especially not one to Mary.

–

The days went by quickly. Lucifer wasn't allowed outside the castle grounds, in case the war came to their town. To pass the time, Lucifer would continue his sword training, but by himself. Since Castle Gruppen was so far north, news rarely came by about the war. In Lucifer's mind, they had to be winning. After all, they had his father, Lenkl Deniere, on their side. Eventually, the days became weeks, and weeks became months, which then became years. It was on Lucifer's eighteenth birthday that the messenger came to the castle.

–

"Charge! For King Bastea!" yelled out General Deniere, as he instructed his men forward. Castle Bastea was under siege and about to fall. The war had raged on for four years and now King Bastea's castle was about to be run over.

The attacking army was led by Dictator-King Ranken; a powerful giant of a man who had assembled a wide variety of cohorts, all brimming with excitement over their newfound power. They were filled with the strongest and meanest soldiers in all of Terre, many of which were part of the new and improved Devil's cult. They all aspired to rule the land with an iron fist, through strength; after all, why should the weak control the strong? The natural order of life was for the strong to survive and the weak to die.

More arrows flew by Deniere's head. *Any volley could be your last. Treat all of them the same.* He raised his shield, which blocked a few from hitting him. Other arrows flew past him or were aimed at other soldiers. He could hear the cries of men who had been hit, some injured, some dying. Deniere ignored all of the background noise; his eyes were set on Sunk Ranken, who wielded a large dane axe. His mission was to eliminate him; everything else was secondary. It didn't matter what he had to do, as long as he could take out Ranken.

Ranken was busy killing a group of Bastea's soldiers when he saw the general charging at him, his horse running at full sprint.

"Deniere's coming! HELP! Archers, fire away!"

Ranken's archer bodyguards took aim, then released a volley of shots towards Deniere. He raised his shield once again, and once again, his shield blocked the arrows. This time, however, a few arrows struck his battle horse, causing it to come crashing to the ground, mortally wounded. Deniere rolled off of his dying steed, gasping for breath. He landed in dirt and mud, his body aching from the fall.

Looking up, the glare of the sun initially blinded his vision. As his eyes adjusted, he could see the archers in the distance notching their arrows, preparing for another volley. He ignored the pain and stood up, then started to head towards them. The archers let loose another volley.

Thud.

Thud.

Thud!

Whizz!

Some arrows hit the shield, while others whizzed by, narrowly missing Deniere. He was now in full stride and was closing the gap fast. He threw his damaged shield at two archers who were bunched together, then decapitated the other two who were desperately trying to reload.

After finishing them off, he went back to the grouped-up archers; one had died from the shield throw, the other crawling back up and trying to notch an arrow quickly. Deniere ran towards the archer; the archer, in a panic, screamed ghoulishly before being stabbed through the chest. The archer's body went limp as blood gushed out of his wounds. Deniere had no time to waste; Ranken, having witnessed what he had just done to his personal guards, had his dane axe ready for combat, ready to kill Deniere.

–

Ranken snarled at Deniere in distaste. Why would such a strong soldier be on the side of the weak? *You'd be alive after today if you listened to me, Lenkl,* thought Ranken. He'd asked Deniere to join him many times, but was always refused. Now, he'd have to kill him. It was a waste of good talent, both on losing Deniere, and the dozens of men that Deniere had already killed of Ranken's.

In the din of the raging battle, the sound of catapults going off, and through the cries of the dying, Ranken and Deniere clashed blades. Both seemed equally skilled and struggled to gain the upper hand. If either fell, the war would surely be over for one side. It wasn't if one lost; it was *when*.

Neither man would leave the area without the other dead.

"Deniere, you fool! You still have one more chance to switch to my side," huffed Ranken, sweating in exertion. Ranken, trying to hide his exhaustion, had an angry sneer on his face. The amount of sweat pouring off his brow might have given him away were Deniere paying attention.

Deniere, unfazed by the comments, ignored him and kept slashing away, fixated on the axe in front of him. He was tired as well; too tired to speak. He could only think of slaying Sunk Ranken, the Dictator-King, and nothing more. With each parry and block, with each cut and slash, his energy faded, his breathing more laboured. As skilled as he was, Ranken seemed to match him. He thought of his wife, his child, his kingdom… everything he had fought for. He *had* to win.

"Might and strength shall rule this land, General. How unfortunate…" said Ranken, jumping back. He was now grinning from ear to ear, as if he'd already won.

"...that you will not live to see it."

Deniere felt a blade pierce through his back plate. He quickly turned around; there stood a commander of Ranken's, who had plunged a sword into him. Deniere had been backstabbed by a third party in the heat of the duel; a dirty tactic, but in war, there were no rules. Deniere fully swung around and sliced the commander in two.

Behind him, Ranken seized his opportunity. He swung his dane axe into the side of Deniere, slashing through his armour and cutting into his torso. Deniere's body went limp as loads of blood gushed out of his wound. Licking his lips in satisfaction, Ranken rejoiced. He could finally rest; his nemesis was finally slain. With that, the rest of the siege would go smoothly. The kingdom of Terre would finally be his!

—

"General Deniere of Northern Terre is dead!" panted the messenger. He gulped nervously before continuing his message. "The war is over... King Bastea was also slain, and Dictator–King Ranken now rules all of Terre."

Upon hearing this news, Mary's fragile figure shuddered; she couldn't handle this news. As she collapsed, the castle maids rushed to her aid. Tears formed around her eyes as the dread and uncertainty slowly crept in. What would happen to them? The world was such a cruel place—a great evil was now in power. As she sat crying, she prayed. She prayed for a better future, a better world. She prayed that God could hear her cries of agony; she prayed for Him to save them.

Oh Lord in heaven, if you can hear my cries; save us from this calamity!

CHAPTER 4

The kingdom changes

Mary was tending to the crops in the field. The afternoon sun was hot; it blistered her pale skin. But she continued, knowing that she had no other choice. Slaves who did not complete their duties for the day were flogged. It was a far cry from what she was used to, but she did it without complaint.

After the war ended, when Bastea fell, King Ranken sent over his own men to control each territory of Terre. In Northern Terre, the Deniere family was replaced by a Baron Wehr, one of Ranken's top commanders in the war. Mary Deniere and her son Lucifer were no longer part of the royalty and were now slaves under the Baron. They worked long hours under the sun, tending to crops, chopping down trees, and doing other menial jobs. It was a difficult and certainly different life from what they were used to but one they were forced to do now, whether or not they liked it.

"There, that's done," whispered Mary to herself. She had finished her allocated section for the day and could now conserve what little energy she had for the next day's toil. She picked up her tools and headed back to the slave's resting area. It was under a tree, decorated with an old table and some wooden chairs that were falling apart.   The tree used to be an apple tree when it was alive; it had soon died under the care of Baron Wehr, who thought his slaves would eat the apples on the tree before he could collect them. There, in the shade of the tree, she saw her son, who had finished his farm work a while ago.

"Lucifer!" she shouted. Lucifer looked up and saw his mom calling for him. He gave her a brief wave, then stood up to walk over to her.

"Mom, don't be too loud. Otherwise the foreman will hear," he said. He knew his mom knew, but one could never be too careful these days.

"I know, darling. But it's your twentieth birthday today! I have a present for you." Mary shuffled around her pockets. The present was some-where in there, but she couldn't find it immediately. *It must have shifted around here somewhere,* she thought. After a few seconds, she found what she was looking for. Smiling at Lucifer, she pulled out a tiny carrot.

"Ta-da! A carrot!"

While her grin was wide, Lucifer knew she was sad inside. In his childhood days, presents were far grander. But now, as lowly slaves with no money, a carrot was the best his mother could do. Even so, Lucifer couldn't take it. His mother looked even skinnier than he did; she probably needed the carrot more.

"You keep it, mom. You need it more than me," he said. He closed his mother's hand for her, handing the carrot back. His mother's smile faded as she spoke to him.

"But Lucifer, you must have a present for your birthday. You must…" She peered into his eyes, but saw nothing inside. Lucifer shook his head once more, then stepped forward and gave his mother a big hug.

"Your present will be this hug then, mom."

As they stood together, Mary had a tear in her eye. Even now, her son was so kind. She had raised him well. But the tear wasn't that of joy; it was of sadness. As his mother, she had failed him.

—

Lucifer was chopping down trees with a dull axe. It was winter; the castle needed firewood. Baron Wehr was planning a feast soon, and needed the castle to not only be warm, but to be brightly lit. Lucifer had on him threadbare clothes, causing him to shiver.

Chop...

Chop...

Chop...

He wiped away the sweat from his forehead. Even in this cold, he was sweating. Snow had started to fall again, too. It was getting colder. He looked to the sky, and saw dark clouds forming in the distance. *A blizzard.*

The pile of wood was large enough. It was his final one of the day; he could finally rest. He loaded up the remaining wood onto a sled, then hauled it towards the castle.

The trek back was uneventful. There was barely anyone outside; the cold had made everyone, even those not done with their chores, flee inside. They'd rather take the flogging than freeze to death in the coming blizzard.

Once he had unloaded the wood to the woodpile, Lucifer headed towards the slave resting quarters. The only part of the day he looked forward to was here, when he could rest and talk to his mother.

But to his dismay, his mother wasn't there. *Probably still cooking for the castle,* he thought. He yawned. His body was tired. He could see her tomorrow, anyhow. He went to sleep on his deer hide cot, blissfully unaware of what had happened.

—

The next day, he had looked in the usual places for Mary: the garden, the kitchen, the slave lounge. She was nowhere to be found. Questioning the other workers and slaves there also produced no results, as no one else had seen her, or admitted to seeing her. After making sure that she wasn't in any of the aforementioned places for the third time, he went to the foreman.

The foreman, an Ofh Sanu, wasn't exactly cruel, but he wasn't nice either. He was there to make sure the slaves were working on time and everything was in order, and sometimes got power hungry, ordering people around for his enjoyment. In any case, he'd likely know the location of Mary, as it was his job to know.

It was late in the evening when Lucifer had finished his chores and was able to walk up to the foreman. The foreman was sitting in a large, fancy seat, writing down something on a piece of paper. Lucifer, being able to read, saw that it had names on it. He didn't recognize any of the names on the page; but oddly, they were all female names.

The foreman, clearly unaware that Lucifer had entered, kept scribbling down names. Lucifer cleared his throat; the foreman jolted back a bit, surprised by someone's presence. When Lucifer caught the foreman's eye, he began.

"Foreman Sanu, sir, do you know where Mary went?" asked Lucifer, in a meek voice.

The foreman looked at him, eyeing Lucifer up and down. After a moment of inspection, the foreman answered. "Mary... your mother Mary?

Hm... I think she and a bunch of other girls got sent off to Ranken's."

"To Bastea? What for?" Lucifer wasn't liking where this was going. Why did King Ranken need her? They were just lowly slaves, after all. It couldn't be because...

The foreman shook his head as he replied to Lucifer. "Ah… probably as sex slaves or summat like that. Ranken might keep some for himself, might sell off others. Probably will make a healthy profit from that, ya know? Unfortunate for you, kid."

—

On my twentieth birthday—the sword and armour. Lucifer's mind raced, thinking back to that day his father showed him the secret room. He had to save his mom. He had to do something. The room behind the gold door! His weapons and armour were in there, left for him by his father before he left for the war.

However, Lucifer still didn't know the code for the lock; without it, he'd have no weapon. Also, there were lots of guards in the castle. They'd surely attack him on sight if he was spotted. But the time to act was now. He wasn't a kid anymore; he couldn't rely on others to solve the situation. He would have to do it himself. The situation was only going to get worse with time, not better. So, the sooner he could get his gear, the better.

–

Mackintosh sat in his cell, scribbling away a game he was playing by himself. Cross the x's over here, the o's over there. It was all he did, for he had nothing else to do. As he scratched the dirt floor with his stick, he pondered. When was Baron Wehr going to execute him? Maybe he forgot about him. Mackintosh wasn't too important, he was just a sergeant. He stifled a cough. The air was musty; dry. He was only allowed one cup of water a day, so his throat was always parched.

Step...

Step...

Step...

Someone was walking down the old wooden stairs of the dungeon. Mackintosh could easily recognize the sound, as that usually meant food was coming. As it was night, however, the sound could only mean inspection. Mackintosh quickly erased his scribbles and then sat over his stick. The guards would probably take away his stick, the only thing that kept him company in the prison, if they found out he had it.

"Uncle Mack?"

The voice was familiar... General Deniere? No, he died two years ago... it couldn't be him. Uncle? Who used to call him Uncle? He had no children of his own, and didn't have any living family either.

"Uncle Mack!"

Mackintosh looked up and peered at the person standing on the other side of the prison cell. It was a familiar-looking face—one he'd seen many times   before.

"Who are you?" whispered Mackintosh. He was confused. He should know this person, but his memory was fuzzy. Too much time spent alone in the cell, he thought. Maybe this was a dream.

"Uncle Mack, it's me, Lucifer. Don't you remember me?" said Lucifer. Mackintosh looked very unkempt, had a scraggly beard, and his clothes were old and torn. *He must've been in here for quite a while,* thought Lucifer. *That may have messed up his mental state.*

Mackintosh's eyes sparkled as he finally realized who it was. It was the son of his friend and general. It was Lucifer Deniere, the rightful ruler of Northern Terre. Mackintosh stood up, albeit slowly, to greet him.

"Little Lucifer, how you have grown. You're taller than me now! Ah, how the years have passed. But what are you doing here? No one is allowed in the prison," said Mackintosh. He looked around, wary. Inspections were very rare these days. Nothing ever happened, so the guards became much more lax; they were probably sleeping at the moment.

Lucifer examined the prison lock. There was no way he'd be able to open it without the key. He looked back to Mackintosh, then asked, "Did my father ever tell you anything? Something about numbers? I need information to get my gear."

Mackintosh racked his brain. His memory was already fuzzy—chances that he'd remember something Deniere said to him long ago? Not very likely. *Numbers, numbers. Something about numbers…*

'*Sergeant, you are in charge of Gruppen's defense while I am gone.*'

'*Yes, sir!*'

'*And one more thing. Do you remember the*

day I found my son?'

'*Yes, sir. The day I heard little Lucifer crying in the forest, sir.'*

'*Remember that date for me, Mack. Promise me you will remember.'*

'*I will, sir."*

"February… second… two hundred…!" Mack sputtered out. Of course he would remember; it was a promise to his lord. That day, the second day of the second month of the two hundredth year, was when Lucifer was found. Mack continued his thoughts. "'Twas the day you were found in that forest, Lucifer. I suppose your father never got to tell you. You're not bound to him by blood…"

Lucifer was taken aback by all the news at once. He wasn't related to his parents by blood? That would explain them looking slightly different. That day wasn't even his birthday, either. His parents must've guessed when his real birthday was and gave that to him. But Lucifer didn't have much time to spare; he could mull over his thoughts later. Now was the time for action. He nodded his thanks to Mackintosh, then left the prison. He had to get his weapons and armour quickly before the guards woke up.

After Lucifer left, Mackintosh picked up his stick and started to draw on the floor again. *X's and o's, make 'em five in a row. Do it five times, then you'll get a bow!*

CHAPTER 5

Devil's arms

Lucifer had to sneak past a few guards to get to the gold door. Luckily for him, most of them were fast asleep, accustomed to the monotony of life in Castle Gruppen. The citizens living in Gruppen were all scared of Baron Wehr; as such, the guards were not needed for much else other than to look intimidating.

Just as he had remembered it, the diamond and gold door was very heavy. Lucifer put his back into it and shoved. It moved slowly at first, then gave way easily around halfway.

The room looked like it did all those years ago; it was a bit dustier than he had last seen it, perhaps a bit smaller too, but it was otherwise the same. There, on the table, lay the dark-silver sword in its glass case. To the right of the table was the suit of dark armour, embroidered upon it the insignia that his father wore; the Deniere family symbol.

Lucifer approached the table and set his eyes on the lock's rotary code. It was all set to zero. It hadn't been touched since his father set it all those years ago.

Alright… two, two, two. Lucifer set the code and waited. Nothing happened. He furrowed his brows. *I need to move the case too.* He placed his hands on the glass case, then pulled up. With a low-pitched creak, it moved up, letting the sword breathe fresh air for the first time in years.

The sword was a beautiful mixture of black and grey-silver. The tip was angled, pointed to the rear; the length of the blade sharp and single-sided, other than the tip's false edge. The hilt and guard were simple and unadorned. Aside from the great length of the blade, the sword seemed very unassuming.

With this blade, thought Lucifer, *I will avenge my father and save my mother.* He grasped the giant sword and tested it out. It was weighty, far heavier than the regular infantry sword he practiced with as a kid. But he could easily handle it; the sword motions came back to him as if he'd never stopped practicing. Now, he'd just have to put on his armour, then his plan could be set in motion.

—

Baron Wehr was holding a large banquet for his esteemed guests that night. It was extravagant, but something the Baron did often. *Too lavish,* thought Lucifer, *while the rest of us starve and live as if we're worth nothing.*

Lucifer was high up on the third floor, observing the banquet from above. Looking down upon the partygoers, the mood of the banquet was cheerful and lively. Unbeknownst to the people in the dining hall, however, was the knight watching them from above. Lucifer would wait until the Baron finished and went to his room. Then, he'd confront him there.

–

"Yeah, yeah. Don't hesitate to visit my castle later!" shouted Wehr, in a festive mood. He waved his guests goodbye, then started to walk to his room. He didn't always live like this. He was raised by cultists until Bastea killed off the original Devil cult. Then, when Ranken called for warriors, Wehr and his brother Behr joined him; the Gweitt brothers had always envisioned their revenge on King Bastea. They also liked the idea to rule the kingdom through strength. They were stronger than others, and as the natural order of life, they should conquer the weak. His exploits during the war earned him this pretty piece of land, although it was pretty cold during the winter. He couldn't complain though, as he was always warm inside the castle and had plenty of slaves to do whatever he wanted. It was the life he had always dreamed of.

Done with the banquet and tired, he waddled back towards his sleeping quarters. He had gotten fat over the years; he no longer had to fight to survive, and he also ate quite a bit more than he probably should. The guards, most of which were half-asleep, quickly jumped to attention as he passed by. *Lazy men,* he thought. *Bah, whatever. Not like anything happens here anyway.*

–

Wehr shooed the maid off with his hand, nonchalantly. She quickly dressed back up, then shuffled out of the room. Wehr chose a different maid every night to sleep with. The more variety, the better. In return, the maids who were chosen would get an extra bowl of gruel for the day. After all, if the maids were too skinny, Wehr might crush them with his weight while having sex with them. With the door now closed, he wandered back to his bed and tried to go to sleep. But there was a cold draft coming from somewhere. *The balcony? I don't remember leaving the balcony open. This damn Gruppen winter,* thought Wehr. He looked at the balcony door and saw that it was wide open. Sighing in frustration, Wehr got back up and then sauntered over to fix the problem.

"Baron Wehr. I heard you sent my mother off to Ranken as a slave."

Lucifer stood on the balcony, his long, dark-silver sword raised and pointed at Wehr's neck. Wehr's eyes went wide as he struggled to piece together a sentence.

"Uh-uh-ss… uh… who-who are you?" There was a towering knight in front of him, one that he had never seen before. The knight's sword glistened in the moonlight, reflecting the moon's amber glow back to him. The knight was dressed in black metal armour; the sight was terrifying.

"I am no one."

With that stated, Lucifer rapidly thrusted his sword forward. It went cleanly through Wehr's neck, decapitating his head in an instant. Lucifer flicked the blood of the Baron off his sword, not before admiring the dark red tint the blood gave the blade. One thing was done, but he couldn't hesitate. Who knows what his mother had been through, or what was being done to her now? He'd need to find a way out of Gruppen, then quickly travel to Castle Bastea.

"Baron Wehr—"

The guard's jaw went wide in surprise. The baron lay on the floor, headless. A giant pool of blood, leaking from the baron's body, was slowly spreading, staining the white carpet a dirty red. Standing behind the dead baron was a tall knight in dark, menacing armour, a giant cape, and a long, bloody sword. For a moment, both of them stood still, staring at each other. Then, the knight lunged forward, and in one quick motion, sliced the guard in half.

—

"HELP! HELP! ASSASSIN!" a guard screamed. He had just witnessed another guard get sliced to pieces by an unknown knight. The giant knight then turned to him and charged. The guard held up his buckler shield and attempted to block the strike, but the sword split the shield in two and completed its journey inside the guard's body. The guard fell limp as the knight took his sword out of his body and continued on his rampage.

Lucifer slew a few more guards across the hallway, all the while looking for the exit. Soon, the resistance started to fade, as guards realized fighting this monster was futile. Some ran away from the castle, screaming, while others attempted to shout for help.

Reaching the exit, Lucifer stopped for a moment to take in a breath. He knew that if he went outside he'd had to fight more, so he'd catch his breath here before going. He closed his eyes and listened to the outside commotion. He could hear the footsteps of soldiers getting ready for battle, the cries for help, armour clanking. *I'm ready,* he thought. *Aim for the forest and run.*

—

Behr was woken up in the dead of night. Unlike Wehr, he still trained like there was a war; therefore he remained fit and ready to fight at any moment. There was a serious commotion outside; his aide told him an assassin was inside the castle. Was his brother Wehr dead? *Good, I'll have control of Northern Terre then,* thought Behr. This thought caused him to grin. This 'assassin', or whoever it was, just got rid of his brother for him. He'd always wanted to, but was always unsure when to do it, or the repercussion of doing so. Well, now it happened naturally, as it should, so that he didn't need to mull over the thought anymore.

—

Lucifer burst through the castle gates. His 'plan' wasn't going to plan; there were too many guards in his way. It would be a deadly slog to get to safety.

There were two guards behind the gate, both who thrusted their spears at him. He parried one and dodged the other, then cut the first guard. The second regained his spear, and thrust again. Lucifer quickly deflected the spear upwards, then stabbed the guard with his sword, killing him. Hearing more yells, he turned around. There stood more guards, their spears raised.

When Behr came onto the scene, there were dead soldiers strewn across the snow, some already frozen in place. Not only was it the middle of winter, but a giant blizzard had already been brewing. The blood soaked the snow and made it a bright red, decorating the eerie scene, lit up by the bright moon at its zenith. In the middle of the dead bodies stood an unknown knight in horrifying armour. *So he's the assassin,* thought Behr, *this could be tough.*

Behr motioned to his aide, Ayd Desmann. Ayd nodded, knowing what Behr wanted. In case Behr couldn't win, he'd have archers shoot this knight. It was a foolproof plan, especially if they were in the middle of combat—the knight would never see it coming.

–

"Step forth, warrior, and face the great Behr Gwiett!" shouted Behr. The name was familiar; especially the surname. Lucifer knew who it was—it was the brother of Wehr. Behr was a giant who wielded a battle axe. As the second in command of Gruppen after the Baron, Behr was now the leader of Ranken's men here.

Lucifer raised his sword forward, then charged at Behr. Behr deflected the speedy thrust, then raised his knee to smash Lucifer's stomach. The knee hit hard armour instead, causing Behr to grimace in pain. Lucifer took a step back, regaining his composure, then sent forth a flurry of cuts at

Behr.

Unable to block all the slices, Behr took some injuries to his arms and started to bleed. The ground under him started to turn red with his blood. Behr wasn't used to losing; it was new to him.

"STOP! Stop—I can cut you a deal, warrior," said Behr, panting. He was already injured, struggling to survive in only a few seconds of combat. This knight was nothing like he'd ever faced before. He was faster and stronger than any human had a right to be; something about him wasn't *natural.*

Behr continued his plea. "You want this land? You can have it. Be the new Baron. Doesn't that sound good to you?"

Lucifer looked at Behr, trying to look past his outward appearance. Was he telling the truth? Behr wasn't Wehr... but then again, rumour had it that he was worse than Wehr. He had to be lying to save himself. Lucifer hesitated; Behr had his weapon down—the telltale sign he was surrendering.

"*A noble knight does not needlessly kill, Lucifer.*"

"*Why? What if they tried to kill me?*"

"*It matters not, my son. If they've surrendered, they pose no more threat to you.*"

His father's words echoed in his head. Behr was surrendering; or at least, it appeared so. To finish him off would go against what his father had taught him. Slowly, Lucifer lowered his sword. If he truly was in control of Gruppen again, there wouldn't be the need for more bloodshed.

Ayd saw Behr lower his weapon. That was the signal. As instructed, the aide then raised his right hand up high. The archers, recognizing the gesture, knew it was time to fire.

The first few arrows ricocheted off Lucifer's armour. Then, one entered through a gap and punctured his shoulder. Lucifer grunted in pain, but had no time to tend to his wound. Behr was already charging at him, battle axe raised and ready to finish him off.

Lucifer parried the overhead blow, then swung two cuts quickly at Behr's legs. Behr blocked the first one with his axe head, but the second one went through his defense and slashed his leg. Behr cried out in pain and stumbled backwards, unable to control his left leg. Lucifer then thrust his sword into Behr's chest, piercing his armour and killing him.

Ayd raised his hand up again. Behr was dead, so there was no point in holding back the volleys now. The archers notched their arrows at maximum pace and sent arrow after arrow towards the knight.

Many arrows got deflected, but some also made it through Lucifer's armour. He held up Behr's dead body and used it as a shield as he limped towards the forest. The horrid trail of red blood that leaked onto the white snow; was it his or Behr's? There was no time to think. All he could do was keep moving until he got to the forest.

Arrows continued to fly by, some smacking into Behr's body, some ricocheting off Lucifer's armour. With each thud of an arrow, Lucifer braced for the pain that could come. Despite this, he kept moving, step by step, through the heavy snow. *A bit further, and I will be in the clear… just a bit more.*

Ayd frowned. Somehow, the knight was able to survive long enough to make it into the forest. But no matter—he'd surely die soon. If not from the arrows, it would be from the cold. If not from the cold, it would be from the rumoured monster that lived deep in the forest. After all, those who entered the forest never returned. He'd seen it firsthand, as a scouting team who had gone to check it out never came back. Ayd's frown soon switched around as the current situation dawned on him. He was the next in line to rule Gruppen. With Wehr and

Behr dead, he wouldn't be an aide anymore. He'd be the new lord.

—

Lucifer had dropped Behr's body near the edge of the forest when the arrows stopped flying towards him. He kept running deeper and deeper into the forest. The only thoughts in his mind were the arrows, which caused him a lot of pain, and the bitter cold, which was getting worse. The blizzard was picking up steam quickly, and it was getting harder to move by the minute.

Step. Step.

Nothing else was on Lucifer's mind. Was he freezing to death, or was he bleeding to death? Perhaps both. With his head hung low to protect his face from the howling wind, he continued his slog, only able to see the torrent of falling snow in front of him.

Step… step…

This felt familiar to him. Like he'd been in

this situation before. What did they call it, déjà vu? He was sure he'd been here before; somehow, the nearby trees looked oddly familiar.

Step... BONK!

His helmet clanged as it hit the rock wall. Lucifer looked up. In front of him was a stone building, an ancient fort of some kind. *This... I remember this place.* He pushed the wall, and as he had thought it would, it moved. It opened up into a dark but warm area. It was the door to the stone building, the very same one he had stumbled upon eight years ago.

The same candle was there at the end of the hallway, the same wooden door left slightly ajar. Inside the building was warm and comforting, unlike the freezing hell outside. As Lucifer walked through the hallway, he could hear the sound of his blood dripping onto the floor. He ignored it and the pain he felt, focusing instead on each step, and slowly marched on.

Upon reaching the wooden door, he placed his hands on the edge, ready to enter. Then, he paused. The girl that lived here, was she still here? Would she remember him? Her name… wasn't it Luna?

Memories flooded back in: The time he got lost and almost died in the forest. It was the girl who lived in here, Luna, who saved his life. Lucifer looked very different from the child he was back then. But Luna was very nice—surely she'd help him again.

The first thing he saw when he opened the door was the cauldron. It was large and bright, as he remembered. It took up the center of the room, warming up the entire space like a furnace. The next thing he noticed was the multitude of skeletons hanging on the rafters. The first time he'd come here, there were only three. Now, they decorated the entire room's edges, too many to count. Lucifer took a few steps in and looked to the throne seat at the back where Luna would sit. No one was there; the room appeared empty.

Lucifer looked closer at the other items in the room. It wasn't dusty, so she had to have been here recently. Why would she leave while there was a blizzard raging outside? Did she have something important to do?

"Another human looking to kill me, I see..." whispered a voice from behind him. Lucifer spun around in surprise; there was Luna, staring at him, her silver sword at the ready, about to execute a diagonal cut. Under her mask was an inhumanely giant grin, one that he could not see. She spoke quietly, with a dangerous tone in her voice.

"Say hello to the dead for me."

She swung her blade at Lucifer. He dodged backwards, then unsheathed his sword in time to block the follow-up attacks. He was already very tired, and possibly dying from blood loss. Even still, he blocked her attacks, though he struggled to find his breath.

"Not attacking, are we? Too scared to?" laughed Luna maniacally. Her green eyes sparkled in the flickering flames of the cauldron fire. Every human who tried to hunt her was now a skeleton hanging on the building's ceiling. This human would be no different.

Lucifer tried to speak, but was unable to. All his energy was being used to stay alive in the fight; he wasn't sure how much longer he'd be conscious. He'd have to stop Luna, but he didn't want to attack her.

"Oh, the poor hunter is now the hunted. Hahaha!" cackled Luna. She'd heard everything humans had to say before they died. Some would plead, others beg, and the cowardly ran. Whatever they chose, they'd always be dead at the end; their skeletons hung on the ceiling to remind others why not to come here.

Lucifer blocked another one of Luna's

powerful slashes, but this time put some weight behind it. He didn't want to do it, but he had to stop her now. Luna stumbled backwards, surprised at the strength the human had. Even though the human was only blocking, this block had a shove with it as well, and it was quite powerful. Still reeling from the block, Luna stared at the human for a moment, waiting for the counterattack.

Lucifer, seeing his chance, took off his helmet, exposing his face.

"It's me, Lucif…"

He had used up all his energy and could feel his consciousness slip away. As he crumpled to the floor, he saw Luna rushing towards him.

Is this a dream of my past?

CHAPTER 6

Reunion with a She-Devil

The first thing he noticed when he woke up was the ceiling. It was the stone ceiling of the ancient building. Surrounding the edge of the ceiling were many skeletons, just hanging there eerily; trophies of dead bounty hunters who had tried their luck at killing the succubus. His helmet was no longer on his head; nor did he feel the weight of his armour. He turned his head to his left, and the sight that greeted him was all too familiar.

Luna was humming a nostalgic tune while cooking soup by the cauldron. Hearing Lucifer shift around, she turned around and saw him looking at her. Their eyes fixed on each other for a moment before Luna turned back to tending to the soup. Lucifer tried to get up, but felt pain all over his torso.

"Lay down, Luc. You're still very hurt from all those arrow wounds," spoke Luna, softly.

Lucifer laid his head back down on the old blanket. Even after all this time, Luna still remembered him. She'd taken off his armour and bandaged up his wounds. She was still the nice lady who lived alone in the forest... but the human skeletons attached to the ceiling were a little concerning.

—

"Ow," muttered Lucifer, grimacing, as Luna replaced an old bandage with a new one. Some blood had dried up and was making the bandage stick to his skin, causing some pain when it was peeled off.

"There, there. You'll feel a lot better once it's replaced," scolded Luna. After finishing the wrapping, she handed him a bowl of soup. She gazed at him, and gave him a smile.

"It's the same soup from last time, do you remember?"

Lucifer nodded and started to drink the soup. It tasted the same as it did all those years ago. In fact, everything was like all those years ago—except it wasn't. A sense of sadness crept into him, but he shook it off. What mattered now was that he was alive. As long as he was alive, he'd be able to avenge his family.

—

The cold winter days passed by uneventfully. Slowly but surely, his wounds healed up until he could move around without too much pain. Luna told him about all the skeletons. They were humans who wanted to kill her because she was a succubus.

"According to humans, succubi are beautiful ladies who lure men with their beauty. Then we kill them and *eat them,* shredding them apart with our dagger-like teeth. Lovely rumour, isn't it?" said

Luna. She had a wistful look in her eyes, one that conveyed sadness. Glancing at Lucifer, she continued, "The one part they did get right, though, was about the teeth."

She slipped off the mask that had always covered her face, baring her fangs at him; it was then that Lucifer saw the demonic sight. Unlike a human's, her smile continued far wider; almost reaching her cheeks in fact, and her teeth were razor-sharp, more akin to a shark's than a human's.

Luna, seeing Lucifer's eyes widen, whispered, "I supposed these teeth are great for grinding up people too, don't you think?"

Lucifer shook his head, maintaining eye contact with her. He said, "Succubus or human, Luna, you're a good person. You've only been defending yourself. If people only got to know you, they'd see you as more than just a monster."

"A person... you're the only human to ever call me that, Luc. You're so lovely," cooed Luna.

She had a big smile on face, which most people would be terrified of. But it didn't bother Lucifer—rather, seeing her smile made him embarrassed for some reason.

As Lucifer continued to heal, he told Luna about what had transpired over the years. The war against Ranken; his father's death; up until he killed the Gwiett brothers and nearly died. Luna listened quietly throughout, curious about the lives of humans. *Humans can be good, yet so evil,* she thought. As he droned on, her gaze slipped, dropping from Lucifer's face to his shirtless body, which by now had regained most of its muscle.

However, this one is so nice... and so muscled and handsome...

—

Lucifer was tired, but had to stay awake. Luna was sleeping on her throne seat. *I could never sleep while sitting,* he thought while looking at her, *but I supposed you could appear awake if someone comes in.* Luna had told him that for her entire life, she'd have to hide when she slept in case someone tried to hunt her while she was sleeping. Now, with Lucifer there, she could sleep 'normally' and have him keep watch.

He fed another wooden twig into the cauldron, causing it to spring back to life. *Just keep watch, and keep the fire going.* It was another lazy day with Luna, waiting for spring to arrive.

Then, he heard muffled voices outside. Lucifer rushed to the doorway; the owners of the voices came from the entrance direction; from the south wall. He went into the hall, then placed his ear on the outer stone wall.

"Oi! It's gotta be 'er boys. A random fuckin' fortress deep in this here forest?"

"Yeah, it's definitely this 'un. I can feel it."

"Hehe. If the legends are right we'll see a crazy hot bitch in here."

"Yeah, and it's five to one."

"Five to one? May as well be mano e mano. We're the five master swordsmen of Psuert, after all."

"Use math, boys. If we five fight at once, there's only a twenty percent chance one of us falls."

"Is that how the math works out, boss?"

"Yeah, I think so. Unless ye want to solo it, Ben? A fifty-fifty?"

"Uh, no thanks. We'll group up."

"So, how'd we get into this thing?"

Thump, thump.

"Keep kicking the wall, it'll surely go down. Hahaha!"

Lucifer had heard enough. Counting the voices, and listening to their conversation, there were five men. It seemed like they were after Luna, and they were just outside, close to the entrance. They hadn't found the door yet, but it was only a matter of time before they did. He tiptoed his way back to Luna, who was still sleeping.

"Luna... Luna!" whispered Lucifer, fiercely. Luna's eyes slowly fluttered open.

"What is it, Luc?" Luna whispered back. Lucifer waking her up when she was sleeping could only mean one thing... right?

Lucifer pointed to the entrance of the room. He whispered, "Five men are hunting you right now. They haven't found the door yet, but they're kicking at the walls. They'll probably find it soon."

Luna quickly got up and picked up her sword. Lucifer went to grab his gear as well, but was interrupted by Luna. She shook her head. He was still injured, after all. He should not be fighting yet.

"You can't go out yet, Luc. You're still healing," she said. She could see that Lucifer was not happy about that.

"There's five of them. Those aren't good odds." Lucifer was very concerned for Luna; did she really stand a chance against the five master swordsmen of Psuert?

Luna stood firm as she answered him. "Trust me, Luc. I've handled myself all this time. This won't be any different." She gave him a smile before putting on her mask. She'd never fought five expert killers at once, but she had always managed to survive.

—

"Oi! The wall moved here!" shouted Ben. He had been kicking at the left side of the building wall when part of it moved. The others rushed over to see the commotion. Ben kicked it again, and the wall moved a bit more. Feeling emboldened, Ben shoulder-charged the wall, and it opened fully, exposing a dark hallway that was perpendicular to the hidden stone door.

"A door! Well, I'll never—"

Ben was stopped mid-sentence by a long sword, its blade which ran right through his chest.

He looked down, then at his fellow swordsmen before dying.

Luna rushed out, blade drawn and ready, and was charged at by four swordsmen simultaneously. As they reached her, she crouched down, dodging two blades, and blocked the other two with her sword. She quickly cut forward, slashing the legs of the two men who had their attacks blocked. The other two had regained their composure after their miss and swung again. Luna staggered backwards, narrowly avoiding the blades. The men, being master swordsmen, knew they had the momentum now.

Luna sprinted towards the trees; she'd have to split the men up somehow. The two uninjured followed first, trailed by the two injured members. Seeing the succubus run had their morale up high.

"Ben's dead, boys, that means the one of us who would've died has died. The rest of us are safe!" shouted out one. Another shouted back, "Uh, is that how the math works out, boss? She's still alive."

The leader shouted back, "I think so—it doesn't matter anyway! Get 'er!"

—

Luna stepped out from behind a tree and thrust her blade into the leading swordsman's sword arm. He dropped his sword and cried out in pain. She then quickly executed a horizontal cut, removing the man's head from his torso. The next swordsman to arrive slashed downwards at Luna right as she finished the execution.

She barely managed to kill the first when she had to dodge backwards to avoid the slash. This hunter seemed more skilled than the others, and Luna had to desperately parry and block his blows. While doing so, the two injured hunters arrived and joined in the attack. Luna had no choice but to start retreating once more. She ran deftly from tree to tree, attempting to obscure their vision of her.

"Split up! The She-Devil is here somewhere; follow the tracks, anything!" growled Carn. As the boss of the master swordsmen of Psuert, it was up to him to give orders. He'd already lost Ben and Carl. They couldn't give up now and have nothing to show for it. They had to kill the monster, no matter the cost.

From behind him, he heard a cry of pain. Spinning around, he saw the succubus attacking his men. He ran over but was too late; another swordsman, John, had died, and the last one alive was missing his left arm and was about to be killed. Carn jabbed at the succubus with his sword, preventing her from killing his soldier.

"B-boss, my arm! My arm!" cried out the soldier.

"Shut up Feics! Grab your sword with your right arm and keep fighting!" yelled back Carn. The succubus started to run off again. *This cowardly bitch keeps running,* thought Carn. *It'll only delay your fate, nothing more.* He had no time, so he picked up his pace. He had to keep pursuing her so he didn't lose sight again.

—

I... I have to trust myself, thought Lucifer. Luna said she'd be fine; but Lucifer wasn't so sure. All it would take was one lucky strike and she'd fall in battle. He put on his armour and grabbed his sword, then headed towards the building entrance. *Forgive me, Luna. But I must listen to myself first.*

The outside air was frigid. It was still cold, and the snow was still deep. There were two dead men splayed outside the building. Lucifer stepped over them and followed the tracks he could see in the snow. He noticed a lot of blood by the tracks, painting the snow around it red. Lucifer picked up his pace. *Please, don't let that blood be from Luna*

He trekked through the snow for a while before seeing movement in the distance. The figure wasn't so familiar; it was larger than Luna's, one of a man. He ran closer for a better look. It was a man in a fur coat, holding a knife in his right hand. His left sleeve along with his arm was missing, and he seemed to wobble unsteadily. Despite all this, he seemed to be very concentrated on his knife. He slowly moved his arm back, as if he planned on throwing the knife. Lucifer looked to where the man was looking—he was aimed at Luna! Luna was fighting with another swordsman, parrying and swinging blows. Lucifer was too far to hit the man with his sword; he had to think fast, do something, before the knife left the man's hand.

"Ha… ha… die, demon bitch," Feics knew he was going to die soon of blood loss, but at least he'd get the kill. Carn would get the credit, sure, but at least one of them would survive. Hopefully, Carn would say he did something useful. As he moved his arm forward, a giant sword suddenly slammed into him from his side, which lifted him in the air for a moment before slamming his dead body into a tree.

–

"Luna!" yelled out Lucifer as he ran towards her. She had just finished her duel with the final swordsman, slaying him. She turned around and immediately berated him.

"Luc, you're going to get sick! I told you I can handle myself," said Luna. She brought her hands to Lucifer's face, feeling them. They were cold, very cold.

"That guy over there, he was going to throw a knife," pointed out Lucifer, panting in exhaustion. He pointed towards a tree somewhere in the back. Luna looked over and saw Lucifer's giant sword stuck sideways in the tree, with a dead man pinned in between.

"I—I... " Luna was lost for words. This fight was at her limits, and that was proof. She may have died had it not been for Lucifer. She shook her head. *He's right, but... whatever.* It didn't matter much, she didn't need to worry about it. Looking at

Lucifer, she spoke.

"Let's go back home. It's cold out here."

CHAPTER 7

The journey south

Lucifer was mostly healed up. His wounds had healed nicely and he could now wear his armour without pain. Winter was also coming to an end, and with that, the bitter cold. Snow was melting, making traversal through the forest much easier.

Luna helped him suit up his armour. Lucifer would be leaving today for Castle Bastea. She had a bittersweet smile on her face. She was hesitant to ask—but if she didn't, she may never have another chance. It was now or never; she had to do it.

"Luc, um…" said Luna. She paused. Her face was now bright red—she was blushing too much. If he noticed, she'd be too nervous to continue.

"What is it, Luna?" questioned Lucifer. Luna looked away from him, which was unusual. Lucifer pressed her. "Is there something wrong?"

"No... nothing," she said. She hung her head low. She was too scared to say it. Who would think it possible: her, a dangerous succubus, nervous to talk to a human?

But this wasn't any regular human.

Lucifer angled his head down to look at her face. Luna was blushing. She saw him look and turned her head away again. Lucifer then placed his hands around her face and forced her to look at him.

"Speak," he said. He gazed down at Luna; for a moment, they both stood still, and it was as quiet as a mouse's whisper.

Then, Luna whispered to him, a hint of seduction in her voice.

"I want to come with you, Luc. Can a lord such as yourself associate with a lowly succubus?"

She moved forward a bit, still nervous, then gave him an embrace, hoping the action would assist her cause. Her head met his chest; it was warm, yet oddly cold at the same time.

—

They walked alongside the road, heading south towards Castle Bastea. It would be a very long journey by foot, but as Luna had stated, 'the longer we walk, the more we can talk.' She seemed rather cheerful, in fact. In any case, Lucifer kept his eye out on the road to see if any of Ranken's men would pass by.

The orange-yellow of the sky tinting the ground indicated it was late evening when they heard the sound of a horse and cart. Lucifer looked back, towards the clopping of hooves, and saw a merchant in the distance. He got a coin purse ready, preparing to hitch a ride. The purse was given to him by Luna. Over the years, she had collected lots of the round pieces of metal from her dead assailants, many who had been rich warlords, amassing quite a large sum. The amount inside was worth more gold than Lucifer had ever seen in one place— more, in fact, than the amount in his father's treasury. Luna, not knowing or caring how human money worked, gave her purse to Lucifer so he could use it to aid their journey.

It seemed that the currency would be put to good use very soon. Merchants would gladly give rides for coin, as it was basically free money when they were travelling from place to place anyway.

–

"Aye! I see a raised hand," greeted the merchant. A raised hand by a person on the road meant they wanted a ride. An interesting couple was waiting by the road—what looked to be a giant knight and his sex slave. A knight with no horse? Well, it wasn't his job to inquire about such personal matters, especially not from a warrior as dangerous looking as he appeared to be.

"A ride to the nearest town down south. Will two silver cover it?" questioned Lucifer. The merchant, hearing two silver, nodded his head vigorously. "Ah, that would cover two days' worth of travel! I'm an honest merchant, see," said the merchant. Lucifer gave the merchant the coin and then hopped onto the cart. He helped Luna on, then they were on their way south.

"We're headed to the town of Gropl. If you don't know, it's in between Gruppen and Ferstat, see," said the merchant. His name was Bjol Merscheaunt—a wide, charming fellow, and he traversed up and down the kingdom every year. He knew the routes like the back of his hand, though some routes had gotten 'harder' to access in recent years, because of the tax roadblocks Ranken had placed on them.

Surveying the land, Lucifer turned his head back towards Bjol. He asked, "From Gropl to Castle Bastea, how far is that?" Castle Bastea was his end goal, after all. Lucifer had never travelled outside of Gruppen, however, so he didn't know how far it was.

The merchant waved his hand, seemingly indicating the distance with his outstretched limb. He responded, "It's quite far. A week from Bastea to the very edges of the kingdom. So, if we were at Gropl, maybe three to five days by horse and cart, assuming nothing goes awry."

In the distance, Lucifer could make out the lights of a small town. *We're close to Gropl at least,* he thought.

—

The small town of Gropl had one inn. The inn was quite large though, as Gropl was the last stop before Gruppen. As lots of coin flowed through it, it was also quite upscale as well. Bjol stopped his horse and cart there and told Lucifer that he would continue the journey south the next day. For now, he and his horse would need to eat and rest.

Luna had never been inside an inn before and was a bit overwhelmed when they entered. There were a lot of people sitting around, eating their dinner, talking, and drinking alcohol. The people here were merchants, townsfolk, and some soldiers. It was quite noisy; the sounds of chatter filled the room, conveying a lively atmosphere throughout the main lobby of the inn.

"You may order a meal after you book a room!" announced the lady at the counter. The inn was busy, busy enough that they had a new policy to only serve residing guests. To force their customers to fork over more money, of course.

Lucifer quickly replied. "A room that can fit two, please." He looked at Luna. She seemed a bit nervous, especially being around this many people. She caught him looking and cheered up a bit, feigning confidence for his sake. As long as she kept her mask on, no one would notice that she wasn't human.

"As for dinner, I'll get a mixed vegetable broth. And Luna will have..." paused Lucifer, looking at her with a raised eyebrow.

Luna peered at the menu, clueless, unable to read. She looked at Lucifer, then to the counter lady. She nervously spoke. "Um... I'll just get the same one he ordered."

They brought their dinner to the room. Obviously, Luna couldn't eat with her mask on; if people saw her dagger-teeth, they'd freak out. The room allocated to them was quite large; it had two beds, side by side, separated by an oak nightstand that held a lit candle on top. There was a bathroom section within the room as well, something novel to Luna. She was used to cleaning herself with snow or with water from the lake in the forest. She had never used a human bath before.

When they finished eating, Lucifer went out to return the bowls, the delicious soup licked clean. Meanwhile, Luna went to the bathroom to take a bath. The water was warm compared to what she was used to in the forest; it was a lot cleaner as well. As she sat in the bath, she closed her eyes and relaxed. *Tonight will be the night I make my move.*

Her terrifying mouth grew wide into a grin.

–

Lucifer had come back and was now taking a bath himself. Luna sat on her bed, wondering what to do. *We have two beds, this won't work,* she thought. She looked around for anything she could use. The table? No, he'd just move it off the bed. The jar? No, he would just move it—wait, perhaps…

Luna sprung into action, a plan formulating in her head. She took the empty jar from the table and walked over to the sink. Then, she filled the jar with cold water. Once satisfied, she walked back to her bed and poured water all over it. *That'll do,* she thought, rubbing her hands together in satisfaction.

Lucifer had finished cleaning himself and was wiping his hair with a towel. He looked in the mirror, looking at his wounds; his muscled body was full of deep scars. A cruel reminder of the arrows that had once been lodged in there, and the pain he felt during his desperate trek through the forest. With his hair now dry, he put the towel back on a makeshift rack and opened the bathroom door to step out. As he turned left to enter the bedroom, Luna rushed up to him.

"Lucifer, my bed has water in it! The staff in this inn are so amateur, really," she pouted. As she pressed her body closer into Lucifer, he noticed she was only wearing her bra and underwear. She gazed up at him with her innocent green eyes, waiting for his answer.

"Well, I suppose you can take my bed, I'll sleep on the floor," stated Lucifer. He looked at the bed; it was wet, drenched with what seemed like a liter of water. He couldn't really be bothered to complain to the innkeeper about it, as he was pretty tired from the long day and needed to sleep soon.

Luna, apparently unsatisfied with his answer, frowned.

"Then you won't have a bed. I can't do that to you. Hey, what if we share *your* bed?" Her gaze continued to fixate on Lucifer, who was now a bit surprised.

He furrowed his brow as he gave thought, then responded, "I suppose we can take the pillows from your bed to separate us—"

He was cut short by a firm answer from Luna.

"What's wrong with sleeping together?"

Lucifer was taken aback. Perhaps she didn't know the etiquette of humans? He cleared his throat, then answered, "Well, usually people don't share a bed unless they're a couple. You know?"

Luna pressed her breasts into him, making sure he could feel how round and perky they were. Then, she spoke softly.

"Well... then why don't we become a

couple?"

She buried her head into his chest. If he rejected her—said he didn't feel the same way—she didn't know what she'd do. The trip would've been for nothing. Lucifer didn't seem to resist her advances, though. Maybe… just maybe her charm was working.

"Go ahead," said Lucifer, plainly. Luna looked up; Lucifer was looking at her intently. Was this his approval? Whether it was or not, it definitely *seemed* to be so; so she took her chance.

Luna clutched Lucifer's face with her hands, then slowly brought her lips closer towards his. As they kissed, Luna felt his hands run along the small of her back, caressing her. When he took his lips off hers, Lucifer didn't say anything, instead showing his intent with his actions. He carried Luna to his bed, then kissed her again. Luna couldn't believe what was happening; he was taking initiative.

But that handsome face still seems cold...

Her thoughts were interrupted as she felt his hands go to her back and remove her bra. *Right now, that doesn't matter,* she thought. *Fill me with your love, Lucifer.*

—

Luna woke up in the morning to a rooster's call. To her side, still sleeping, was Lucifer. She huddled over him and admired his muscled body. Even with some scars visible, it was still beautiful to her. She ran her fingers through his abs, a terrifying smirk evident on her face.

She still couldn't believe what had happened last night. It did kind of hurt, but she'd expected that. Lucifer was careful with her, briefly stopping when it hurt too much, making sure she was comfortable. Her body shuddered at the thought of doing it again, desperately craving for more.

—

In the afternoon, Lucifer and Luna climbed back

onto the merchant's cart. They would continue their journey south. 'One silver for one day in the horse-cart, see', as Bjol put it. Each day they'd be able to travel past a town or two. To reach Castle Bastea they'd need to make a detour to Eastern Terre, as the entryway between Middle Terre and Northern Terre was blocked off by Ranken's army. It was good for Bjol, though. The capital of Eastern Terre, Psuert, was a thriving place the last time he visited. It would be good for business.

CHAPTER 8

The coward king of Psuert

It took another day of travelling to get to Psuert. Bjol completely skipped Ferstal, the southernmost town of Northern Terre, and headed directly to Zwidal, in Eastern Terre, to trade. There, they spent the night in a regular inn, resting up for the day to come. In the morn, they continued to Psuert; by the afternoon, they arrived.

As the capital of Eastern Terre, Psuert was a large city. It was built near the eastern border, by a large lake, better suited for human settlement as opposed to the majority of Eastern Terre which had swampland or jungle.

Castle Psuert was a wide but short castle. It

was built from hard sandstone, many centuries ago, by its first king. Ever since, it had stood as the most prominent landmark of Eastern Terre, representing itself indirectly—as Eastern Terre was a large but mostly flat kingdom, devoid of hills and mountains.

—

The sun shone down harshly upon them as they came up to the queue of citizens waiting to enter the city. There were two guards standing at the entrance, checking inside the contents of a farmer's satchel. After rummaging through it, the guards seemed satisfied with the results and let the farmer through.

"Bjol, how long will this take?" questioned Lucifer. They were fifth in line, and he'd never had to wait for an entrance queue before.

"Ah, I'd say a minute per person, see," replied Bjol. As a lifelong merchant, he knew all about travelling. Queues were more common now, as the land was restless after Bastea's defeat.

Ranken's lords were very scrutinizing on travellers entering cities; when the war ended, many people were not happy with Ranken taking power, and so militias and rebels alike popped up throughout Terre. The guards were probably checking for hidden weapons. Bjol briefly glanced back at Lucifer. The knight had a giant sword; the lady, as well. The swords weren't hidden, so it shouldn't be a problem as long as they weren't enemies of Ranken. But they weren't, right? Bjol frowned. He'd never asked them, never pried about their past.

"Uh, say, Sir Lucifer, may I ask, which lord do you serve under?" asked Bjol. He needed to make sure they wouldn't cause a commotion when they entered the city.

"I… my lord died in the war. Now I have none," replied Lucifer. He almost said he was the lord of Northern Terre, but stopped himself in time. No one besides Luna would know about his past, he decided, as he was probably wanted by King

Ranken after slaying Baron Wehr.

"Ah. Well, disclose that to the guard when we enter, they'll want to know about your weapons, see," replied Bjol. Looking ahead, the queue was thinning out.

–

"No! Stop! Help!" shouted out a peasant. They waved their arms around helplessly as the guards struggled to put their arms in handcuffs.

"Down, rabble, or do ya want a shank in yer gut?" scoffed the entrance guard.

The peasant calmed down after the threat, and dejectedly accepted his fate. The guards hand-cuffed him, dragged him up by the arms, then led him off.

"See, that's what happens to you if they catch you hiding weapons. Was probably a weapon smuggler," whispered Bjol. The commotion in front of them was unnerving some of the people in the back of the queue, who were now hushedly talking and shifting around nervously amongst themselves.

"The guards left with that fool... I don't see anyone else guarding the entrance," mentioned Luna. She was paying close attention to the entranceway, and noticed no other guards nearby. Her hand brushed a loose strand of hair away from her face as she continued. "Perhaps... we may just walk through?"

Lucifer looked at Luna in surprise. What she suggested would be breaking the rules. Illegal, possibly.

"Eh, might as well. It might actually be less risky than entering while declaring your weapons. We're going in," said Bjol as he lifted up the reins of his horse. The horse trotted along, passing through the entrance to the city.

Once inside the city walls, they could relax again. Going through the entrance was scary but uneventful. No guards were posted there other than the two on the front, and those two were busy locking up the weapon smuggler. A few other travellers in the back of the queue rushed forward to take advantage of the situation as well, not bothering to check in with the guards or pay the entrance fee.

Even though the day was blisteringly hot, many people were bustling around the city doing their everyday tasks. It was quite loud; street vendors were yelling for people to try out their products, soldiers on break were eating their meals, and newsmen were yelling out the latest events in the kingdom.

"Hear ye! Hear ye! Castle Gruppen still remains in turmoil two months after the Baron's assassination! Warlords aplenty fight for control of the capital!" yelled out a newsman. "Multiple war-lords now fight to win the seat for Baron of Northern Terre! The battle for supremacy continues to this day!"

"Sounds like Ranken's men are vying for power there. I feel bad for the people who live there,

there's gonna be a big power struggle for some time until someone comes out on top," remarked Bjol.

Lucifer grimaced, but held onto his thoughts. He was the one who killed Wehr; now it seemed like he put his town in trouble once again. Far from home, there was nothing he could do. He had to ignore it, leave Gruppen to figure it out by itself. For now, he had to focus on saving his mother.

—

Bjol would spend a few days in Psuert to sell his goods. In the meantime, Lucifer and Luna were free to do whatever they wanted while they waited. Lucifer didn't really want to do anything; he was anxious to get back on the road and head to Castle Bastea. Luna, on the other hand, had different plans. She wanted to explore the city; the first one she'd ever been in.

"One candied apple, please."

"That'll be two bronze, good sir."

Lucifer handed over the coins to the vendor, then watched as they prepared the apple. The vendor stuck a wooden stick through it and then spun the apple through a mix of chocolate and sugar. Once content with the result, the vendor handed him the snack.

"Thank you for shopping at Candied Fruits! We hope you visit back sometime!"

Lucifer eyed the apple for a bit, making sure it was safe to eat, then handed it over to Luna. "Here you go, Luna," he said. Luna's eyes lit up as she took the apple. She'd convinced Lucifer to take her out and explore the city. She'd never been to a human city before, and heard of the things they had. Tasty food, magnificent sights; wonderful things for those with the coin to pay for it. At first, he said no, as he didn't want to risk anyone recognizing him or his armour. Tales of the assassin of Gruppen had spread, after all. But when she pouted at him, he retracted his decision very quickly and complied with her tyrannical demands.

Leaving the food stand, they walked about, trying to find a more isolated place. She couldn't eat with her mask on, and she wouldn't take off her mask unless no one was watching. She was a succubus, after all. Her mouth would frighten normal people and they'd definitely call the guards.

"Isn't there a view by the castle of lake Psuert?" questioned Luna, pondering aloud.

"Yes, there is. We'll go there then. Hopefully there aren't many people around," replied Lucifer. It would take some time to get there through the throngs of people in the city, but he thought the view would be well worth it when they got there.

–

"My liege, please stop! Please!" yelled out a guard. He was running after a skinny man who wore green royal robes. The man looked behind him, saw the guard, then picked up his pace. His sandals made a loud slapping noise as he ran, kicking up plumbs of dust and sand after him. Then, he ran into the hooded figure.

The hooded man turned around quickly, startled by the bump. The skinny man had fallen down, bruised from the accident. The figure looked down, and after studying the fallen man for a moment, recognized the robed person. Grinning, he took out his shortsword, hidden underneath his cloak, and dragged the skinny man up. He held his sword to the skinny man's neck as the guard approached, wide-eyed and trembling.

"Don't ye move an inch closer, bucko," warned the hooded man to the guard.

The guard stopped in his tracks and raised his hands up slightly, gesturing a surrender.

"Please don't hurt him. Oh…"

The hooded man grinned.

"Oh? How much for the king? One gold coin and I'll let him go right now," he said, a wicked grin evident on his face.

The skinny, green-robed man was the King of Psuert, who had been under house arrest after the war. He was a meek and mild man, who, instead of resisting Ranken, gave up his power. Ranken had elected a Baron Carn Eje to seize control of Eastern Terre. But weeks ago, Carn and his master swordsmen left on a journey north and hadn't returned.

The king, noticing the swordsmen hadn't come back in a while, had decided to take his chances today. He had run out of the castle to try to escape Psuert. Unfortunately for him, the man Baron Carn placed in charge during his absence, a commander named Geto, saw the king escape. The king had lost his wits and ran through the streets of Psuert aimlessly in an attempt to avoid Geto's soldiers. His bodyguard chased after him in an attempt to calm him down, to no avail. And now it seemed like the king ran into the wrong person; a nefarious sellsword who saw an opportunity in front of them to make some easy coin.

"Uh, uh… I don't have that on me, but I'm sure someone from the castle can get you that, sir!" trembled the bodyguard.

The hooded man frowned. This was obviously a ploy to get more time, maybe call for backup. He needed to do this quickly before any of that could happen.

"No, I need it now. NOW. Or your king dies."

The bodyguard's mind raced, not knowing what to do. He didn't have the coin on him, and he was too far from the hooded man to get the jump on him. His king needed his help, but this time he couldn't save him…

"H-how about you take me as a hostage? I'll lay my sword down," said the guard. He lowered his sword to the ground, hoping the hooded man would listen.

"You fool! Now I can just kill you and take

the king for myself!" laughed the hooded man. He moved the sword away from the king's neck, then pointed it towards the guard. "You're de—"

The hooded man stopped mid-sentence. Confused, the guard looked up, wondering why the hooded man suddenly stopped. Then, he noticed the silver blade sticking out of his neck. The guard screamed and fell onto the ground, shaking in fear. The king, noticing his guard's reaction, slowly turned his head around. A long blade had pierced his assailant's neck and just barely missed his own. The king also screamed, then fell to the ground just as his guard had.

"This guard's as much a pushover as this king is," muttered Luna. She took her blade out of the hooded man's neck, causing his lifeless body to crumple to the floor. She looked down to the huddled figures of the frightened king and guard.

"Well? Where's my thanks for saving your lives?" she demanded, glaring at them intensely.

"Th-th-th-thanks," stuttered out the king. He looked over to the guard, wide-eyed, and motioned with his head. The guard could barely make eye contact with Luna as he spoke.

"Th-thanks for saving my liege, ma'am."

–

Luna had heard the commotion from far away, after only taking a single bite out of her apple. She threw it into the lake, then ran towards the sound, startling Lucifer. As he ran behind her, it took a few moments before he could hear the voices and figure out what was happening. When he arrived at the scene, Luna had already dispatched the would-be murderer, and now appeared to be intimidating the king and his bodyguard.

So this is the king of Eastern Terre. Vakzi Rakcizs, thought Lucifer, *the cowardly king.*

"Apparently you're the king of this place? Why are you running all willy-nilly with a single guard, who seems incapable of guarding even a single peasant?" questioned Luna. On her face was an angry scowl, something that kept the king and his loyal guard from looking at her.

"Uh, I'm more like a puppet king right now, so I don't really control anything... uh... and I'm trying to run away from the guy in charge right now," mumbled King Rakcizs, still trembling in fear. "If I had my commander, I might be able to take back my city, ya know?..."

Luna scowled at him. This king seemed very unsure of himself. *Psh, no wonder he's a puppet king, he has no confidence.*

"I could help you with that," offered Lucifer. He was listening to the conversation carefully. King Rakcizs apparently still had an army by his side, just that they were controlled by Commander Geto. If he could somehow get back in power, his men would surely fight for him, right?

"R-really?" King Rakcizs was surprised. These two scary-looking people had appeared out of nowhere, saving his life. Now they offered to help him win back his kingdom. Was this a dream?

—

"M-my commander, Commander Gronc, is in prison. If he somehow got out, he'd easily get the support of my army back…" mentioned King Rakcizs. The four of them stood outside of Castle Psuert, at a secret entrance by the rear. Rakcizs had used this entrance to escape just a few hours earlier, but it seemed like he was going to have to go back.

"T-the prison's in the basement, I-I guess I can show you the way," mumbled Rakcizs. Outwardly, he trembled in fear, but now was his chance to become king again. He put Gronc in prison when he gave up his throne; it was only right for him to rescue him, now that there was a possibility.

Lucifer nodded to Rakcizs, then spoke. "Lead the way, then. If any guards turn on you, I'll make sure to slay them."

—

As they walked through the echoey halls of the castle, they met no resistance. The guards, seeing Rakcizs, pretended not to see him and continued on with their duties. Commander Geto was out in the city looking for Rakcizs, with his loyal followers. The men left in the castle were Rakcizs', who, while disappointed in Rakcizs, didn't dislike him. Rakcizs was a good ruler, just a scaredy cat who was afraid of war.

"Gronc… Gronc!" yelled out Rakcizs. He peered into Gronc's cell; inside was a man, slumped over.

"Gronc…?"

Was he dead? No, that couldn't be. Gronc was the strongest man Rakcizs knew, which was why he made him commander. It just wasn't possible.

"Uılılılı….."

Gronc slowly lifted his head, moaning, then turned around. His eyes seemed to grow larger as he realized who was talking to him.

"My-my liege! You're here?" whisper--shouted Gronc, incredulous.

"My poor Gronc... let me help you out..." responded Rakcizs, fumbling with the lock. He tried, for a few seconds, to no avail. Frustrated, Luna pushed him aside.

"Allow me," she said, sighing in impatience. She did an overhand cut and shattered the lock. The door, now free, opened loudly with a sound that let them know the cell door had probably not been opened ever since it had been closed.

Gronc rushed out and hugged Rakcizs.

"Oh, my. Poor Gronc, poor Gronc..." muttered the king. Luna and Lucifer looked at each other, awkwardly, then to the bodyguard. The king's bodyguard shrugged. Rakcizs and Gronc seemed a bit closer together than just a king and his commander, but who was a simple bodyguard to say otherwise?

CHAPTER 9

Revolt in Eastern Terre

"Men! The time has come. When Geto comes back, he will be killed, and we shall take back our castle!" thundered Gronc. The soldiers in front of him cheered loudly. Finally, they'd get a chance to fight. They all hated Ranken as much as the next and were eager to get Psuert back into the control of Gronc, by proxy of their king.

"Slay all those who do not accept King Rakcizs as king! Slay all those loyal to Dictator-King Ranken! No mercy!" yelled out Gronc. The cheers went louder this time.

Rakcizs sat on his throne, scared. He'd never been in a war before, nor had his men. They seemed a bit too cheerful for this.

—

"Lame, knuckle-biting, candied-apple eating, son-of-a-bitch whore," sneered Geto. He and his men had searched from dawn to dusk for the escaped puppet king, but to no avail. All he had to show were tired soldiers, a few beat-up citizens who were questioned, and one of his sellswords dead in a back alley. Did Rakcizs kill his sellsword? *Ain't no way,* thought Geto, *Rakcizs is scared of his own shadow.* His contingent was now returning to Castle Psuert unsuccessful. Ranken wouldn't be pleased with this result. *I just won't tell 'em, heh. None will be the wiser. I don't need this puppet king anyway, I can rule the populace through force.* The only reason to keep Rakcizs around was because he was popular with the people. He was nice, too nice—a pushover, some might say. Now that he was gone, Geto could return to his favourite method of rule—through brute force. Execute those who dissented. Public floggings. Sky high taxes. A grin crept up on Geto's face as he realized that maybe Rakcizs escaping was a good thing. Now, he'd get to have his fun.

"No guards in sight, commander!"

A soldier from his contingent woke him up from his thoughts. *No guards? What is this?* Geto looked up at the castle. They had now arrived in front of the main entrance, but indeed, there were no guards in sight. He had definitely seen them when he and his group went out earlier in the day. Something was amiss in the castle, but he wasn't sure what was.

"Onward, march!" Geto led his contingent through the main gate. When he found out who was slacking off, he'd commence the first public flogging. *Perfect,* he thought, *this will show everyone what they can expect from their new leader.*

The first soldier to go down was right in front of him. The soldier fell backwards, off of his horse, clutching an arrow that was embedded in his chest. Geto immediately rolled off his horse just before an arrow whizzed past where his head was a moment before. As he brought his shield up, he saw the castle guards stream out, charging at his force. *Curse you, puppet-king,* he thought. *I will kill you!*

—

"Charge! CHARGE!" yelled Gronc, his halberd raised. He, along with his men, rushed forward towards the mass of soldiers that belonged to Geto. Luna turned to Lucifer, unsure of what to do.

"Do we go? Or do you think they got this?"

Lucifer pondered for a bit, then spoke his mind.

"Those men belong to Ranken… it wouldn't hurt to help remove them from Psuert," he said. He unsheathed his blade, then looked to Luna.

"Don't fight if you don't want to. It's not your fight. It's mine, however, so I will do what's necessary." With that, he leaped into the fray.

—

Geto blocked the soldier's overhand attack with his shield, then countered with a stab to their stomach, killing them. He threw the body off, just to have another soldier come swinging their sword. *Just how many are there?* thought Geto. *We are out-numbered here… everyone turned on us.* Indeed, everyone that remained at the castle was loyal to Rakcizs, and they had all turned out for the battle against Geto and his men. To fight while out-numbered wasn't smart. Geto had a better plan. He'd go after their leader; without a king to fight for, would Rakcizs' soldiers continue to fight? Or would they give up?

–

Rakcizs was in the throne room, sitting on the floor. He had his hands on his head, waiting for the battle to be over. He could hear the cries of men fighting outside; some cries of anger, some of battle fury, others of dying men. *I'm such a coward,* he thought, *I should be out there with my men.* Rakcizs had never trained with a weapon before, however, so he'd be useless there. Besides, Gronc told him to stay here, where it was safe. If Rakcizs died in battle, who knew what would happen to his soldiers' morale.

Suddenly, the main door flew open. In came Geto, blood dripping from his sword, a menacing look on his face. He had managed to sneak his way into the castle amidst the chaos and cleaved through the guards in the hallway. Looking around, he spotted Rakcizs, cowering on the floor. There was only one guard remaining between him and the coward king. A large grin took over Geto's face. The mightiest always win—and Geto was far mightier than Rakcizs.

"Commander Geto! B-back away from t-the king!" yelled out the lone guard. He stood in front of Rakcizs, sword drawn and ready. He turned his head around and looked Rakcizs in the eye.

"D-do not worry, my liege. I will prot—"

The bodyguard stopped abruptly; blood started to pour out of his mouth. Geto took his sword out of the guard's body then slashed at it again, causing more blood to flow out. The bodyguard slumped to the throne room floor, staining the elegant designs on the ground with blood.

Rakcizs spoke not a word, but only stared at Geto. He was going to die here. He lived a comfortable life, but as a coward. Was this his legacy? His trusty bodyguard—Tom was his name—remained loyal until the end.

I... I can't die a coward. I must do something...

Rakcizs stood up, slowly. Geto laughed; what was this fool doing? Rakcizs had no weapon, no way of fighting back. Was the cowardly king actually going to do something for the first time in his life?

"Standing up to say your final words, Rakcizs?" sneered Geto, a smug grin on his face.

Once fully stood up, Rakcizs slowly turned around. Geto was confused; did he want to get stabbed in the back? What a pitiful way to die, not even facing his killer. This king was the ultimate coward; he didn't have any dignity, not even in his final moments. *Well, time to end this.* Geto swung his sword back, preparing to stab the king. Then, the king bolted for the door.

–

Luna was on the second floor of the castle, watching the battle take place through a window. *Humans will gladly give their life for what matters to them,* she thought, *and also for things that matter not at all.* Her eyes came upon Lucifer, who deftly slew hoards of Geto's men with seemingly little effort. *He can't be human, not with his strength and speed.* The battle would soon be over, and it would be a resounding victory for Gronc's forces.

Pit pat, pit pat…
Pit pat pat pat…

Luna's ears pricked up, hearing the sound of footsteps. It seemed to come from the stairway; it was coming closer to her. Was someone running up? An enemy, perhaps? She stepped back from the window and poked her head out in the hallway to see who was running.

There was Rakcizs, sprinting over the stairs, three at a time, his leg bleeding from a cut. He stumbled over the last step then clambered back up and ran towards Luna, desperation in his eyes. Not far behind him was Geto, running after the king like a madman, blood dripping from his sword.

"H-...huelpf..." mumbled Rakcizs. He lost his footing on the slippery marble floor, then fell to the ground with a hard *thump.* Luna drew her blade and sprinted towards the fallen king.

Geto's sword almost struck Rakcizs, but the blow never came. Luna parried the attack then knocked Geto back with her right foot, sending him flying backwards. The winded commander hastily got back up just in time to block her follow-up attack. *Who is this devil of a lady, and why is she so strong?*

Geto struggled to block all her attacks, but was seemingly just outmatched. Her slashes and blocks were blindingly quick, something Geto had never seen, not even in the war. She was unlike any fighter he'd faced before. *This must be who Rakcizs found... a mercenary, but paid with what money?*

Luna stepped back, preparing for a stab. Her foot landed on something squishy—

"OW! That's me, Lady!" cried out Rakcizs, still on the floor.

Luna looked back. Her right foot was on his chest, crushing him. She quickly lifted her foot up and relocated it to a better position.   Geto, seeing his chance, swung his arms back and then swung forward his sword as hard as he could.

Luna blocked the attack, but fell down to the floor due to the force of the blow. Their swords clashed as Luna struggled to get back up, but was unable to because of Geto's weight.

"You're dead now, wench. I am the mightiest warrior of them all!" shrieked Geto. He swung again and again, only to be blocked by Luna. But he could see that her strength was waning from each blow, so he kept up the pressure, swinging again and again. He had trained for years and fought in both wars. He was a hardened commander, the best fighter in the town he'd grown up in. He'd win this just as he won all those other times.

–

"The battle is won!" cried out Gronc. His men cheered loudly. The castle grounds were filled with Geto's dead soldiers, who, outnumbered, struggled to damage Gronc's masses of soldiers. To add to that, Sir Lucifer had rushed into the middle of the contingent and mowed down soldiers as if they were nothing but mere flies on a wall. Now all they had to do was reconvene with Rakcizs, and Psuert would be under its rightful ruler once again.

—

Rakcizs held onto Geto's leg, causing him to momentarily stumble. "Lady, you must—"

Geto swung his sword around, slashing Rakcizs. The king groaned in agony, but he had finally done something in his life. He wouldn't die a coward. *Go on, Lady Luna. You must defeat Commander Geto...*

Luna finally had a moment to stand up. She pushed her weary body up with her left hand, then slashed downwards at Geto. Geto blocked the first hit, but was unable to swing his sword around for the second. The second slash sliced off his off-arm. Geto dropped his sword instinctively to clutch at the bloody stump, screaming in pain. Luna thrust her sword into his stomach, then pulled it back out quickly, dragging along with it contents of his insides. Geto let out a ghoulish moan before going limp.

–

"King? King Rakcizs!" screamed Gronc. The hallway and throne room had only dead bodyguards; Rakcizs was nowhere to be found. Gronc and his men had run around the castle searching for their king. Now on the second floor, did they finally witness the bloody scene in front of them.

Luna hovered over Rakcizs, wrapping his bloody body around with a cut-off piece of his royal robe. Commander Geto lay dead nearby, who was the host of the horrific sight of blood and guts which were strewn out of his insides.

Gronc rushed to Rakcizs and knelt down to him. He cried out, "Oh, Lady Luna. Pray tell me he's okay… please."

Luna, now done bandaging up the king, responded. "He has a cut on his leg and on his chest Both aren't too deep, so assuming he doesn't die of fright from seeing our man Geto over there, sure."

Rakcizs opened his eyes, spotting Gronc.

His mouth moved, as if he wanted to say something. Then, he spoke.

"Commander… before I pass on… there is something I want you to know…" muttered Rakcizs, his voice croaking.

Gronc, with tears in his eyes, started to cry for reasons unknown to anyone else in the room other than himself..

"I've… I've always loved you, Gronc Grenada."

CHAPTER 10

Ranken, the Dictator-King

Lucifer and Luna were off to say their farewells to the king and his men. King Rakcizs had insisted that they could stay—they were now honorary royal members after what they'd done for his kingdom. Whatever they wanted, he could supply them. But with his mother still out there, Lucifer had to go. With teary eyes, the king bid the two warriors good-bye.

"Remember, Sir Lucifer, Lady Luna, you two are always welcome back to Psuert. You've helped me reclaim my castle and saved my life multiple times," said Rakcizs.

"Sometime in the future, perhaps, when all

is said and done," replied Lucifer. Luna nodded in agreement. For now, Lucifer's mother remained to be saved.

Gronc, who had been holding Rakcizs' hand, went down to the floor and knelt.

"Oh, Lady Luna. I thank you from the bottom of my heart. You've saved my dearest two times now."

Luna shifted around nervously, not sure how to take the compliment. "Stand up, commander. You're looking a bit pathetic right now."

Gronc stood back up hastily. He said, "Oh, of course, of course. I must look the part of a commander no matter the situation!" Brushing his pants off, he continued. "If not for you two though, I doubt King Rakcizs would have ever confessed to me. So for that as well, I also thank you."

—

"From Eastern Terre to Castle Bas-tea we go! Closin' around the corner like we're from Pan-gea!"

sang Bjol. They had made good progress; they had already passed by Renast, the town between Psuert and Castle Bastea, and were set to arrive at Castle Bastea by the late evening. Bjol had made a lot of money in Psuert and was in a good mood. Once there, the merchant and the warriors would part ways, as Bjol would continue south to trade, while Lucifer would search for his mother, Mary.

—

The bell of Bastea rang twenty-one times, signalling the new hour which had come. The gates closed at twenty-two hours, so they made it with an hour to spare. As they approached the guards, Bjol reminded the two of what to say.

"Remember, don't hide ya weapons, make it clear that you're a knight, yadda yadda."

Lucifer nodded. It was his third time hearing this, but Bjol was rightfully nervous. Castle Bastea was the center of the kingdom, as well as its capital. Inside the castle was where the ruler of

Terre sat—currently Dictator-King Ranken. The castle and its surrounding territory were heavily guarded from bottom to top, especially as the number of rebels grew.

–

The guard sneered at the peasant. The castle was filled with enough commoners already; they didn't need *this* person. An extra peasant added no value to the castle. *Probably a rebel spy,* he thought. With a flick of his wrist, he rejected the peasant from entering. The peasant wept as he turned around and left, his hopes of getting a safer life in the castle ruined.

"Next!" called out the guard. It was a merchant, but that wasn't what interested him. On the cart were a knight and his maiden; something you didn't see every day. *This guy looks kind of scary,* the guard thought, *looks like someone Dictator-King Ranken would associate with.*

The guard eyed the large swords that were sheathed by both the knight and the lady. It was very unusual for a woman to be carrying a sword.

"The wench, why does she need a weapon? Wenches cannot be knights," belittled the guard. The lady remained silent, as she should be. The knight responded to him promptly.

"Aye, she carries my backup sword for me. Why bother carrying it when I can get my slave to do it for me, eh?"

The guard smiled. This knight was a smart one, indeed. He nodded in agreement. "Well, everything checks out. Go on in, now. Enjoy Castle *Ranken*."

—

As the cart bumped through the stone road towards the inner realm of the castle, Luna nudged Lucifer on his arm, getting his attention.

Master, what shall I do for you today? Would you like a shoulder massage? A glass of wine, perhaps?" she joked, a smile evident under her mask.

"Luna..." replied Lucifer, exasperated. Every once in a while she'd come up with jokes about it. Despite his best efforts to not entertain it, she'd randomly start fussing over him, pretending that he was her master.

"Oi!" shouted Bjol. "We're here!"

They had reached Bastea Inn.

—

Bjol bid them farewell then rode off to continue his journey. He was going to go south to Southern Terre, then he'd go to Western Terre after that. It was a merchant's life, one that he had always lived. Lucifer tipped him a few extra silver, surprising Bjol. *A good man, that one,* thought Bjol as he left, *I'll miss their chatter in the back during these long trips.*

—

Once they booked a room, they devised their plan. Lucifer would go to where the slaves were auctioned and try to find his mother. If she was already sold, he'd try to find log books or something of that nature. Luna was free to do whatever she wanted. As expected, she chose to stick with Lucifer.

The auction opened at noon. There were men and women up for sale; they looked scrawny, dishevelled, and kept their eyes on the ground. Lucifer peered around, looking for his mother. She did not seem to be anywhere in the area. Moving up, past the crowd of interested buyers, Lucifer spotted a man with glasses holding a log book, who was marking down the sales. Motioning for Luna to follow, he walked over.

"Excuse me."

The man looked up from his book, peering at Lucifer. He narrowed his eyes, seemed to scan him, then responded. "Ahem. What do you want, sir?"

"I'd like to see logs of a slave trade, possibly months old by now. Surely that's possible?" asked Lucifer.

The man twiddled his fingers for a bit before smiling. He pushed his glasses up a bit, adjusting them for no apparent reason, before replying.

"Anything is possible for those with coin."

Lucifer retrieved the coin purse and took out a silver. He handed it over to the man. The man inspected the coin for a moment; once satisfied, he rummaged through his bag before pulling out a very large book.

"This one has all of 'em for the current year," said the man, handing it over. "Do return it once you are finished."

Lucifer took the book, thanked the man, then walked back with Luna to a nearby bench..

A few minutes passed by as Lucifer read the contents of the logbook. Luna couldn't read, so she peered at the auction, watching the humans sell and trade their own kind. *Humans are nasty to their own kind too,* she thought, *evil beings, the lot.*

Then, Lucifer nudged Luna.

"A Mary Deniere was sold to a Count Mizo Creiz in Khaeru, a month ago. That has to be her."

Luna furrowed her eyebrows. "Khaeru? Where's that? Are we going to have to travel again?"

Lucifer nodded, then explained. "Khaeru is the northernmost city of Southern Terre, and is its capital. So yes, we'll need to travel again. There are travel carriages here we can use, but they can cost a bit."

Luna shrugged, unfazed. "Whatever, just pay for it. We should get going."

—

As they walked to the travel agency, a loud horn blared in the distance. Soon after, a thundering voice could be heard.

"HEAR YE, HEAR YE! DICTATOR-KING RANKEN HAS GRACED THEE WITH HIS PRESENCE! MOVE ASIDE FOR HIM AND THE

KING'S GUARDS!"

Lucifer, who towered over the general populace, scanned the area. In the distance, he spotted a group of heavily armed soldiers; in the middle of the caravan was a large, fancy carriage, with an armoured figure inside.

Luna, only being of average height, was unable to see what was happening. She tugged at Lucifer's arm with a questioning look in her eyes.

"I think that's Ranken in the middle of the caravan... he's doing a parade or something," said Lucifer. As the parade moved closer, the smell of fear hung in the air. The citizens of Castle Bastea were scared of Ranken, their new ruler.

Luna tugged at Lucifer's arm again, bringing him back to reality. "There's nothing we can do about him right now, right? Let's go."

Lucifer nodded; it was true. There was no way to confront Ranken right now. He was just a single knight, and Ranken had a castle full of his men surrounding him. For now, he'd need to focus on his adoptive mother.

Mother—tomorrow, I will save you.

CHAPTER 11

Fated to never come

They entered Castle Khaeru without trouble. They had purchased the luxury travel plan, so their carriage was large and fully protected them from prying eyes. The guards at Khaeru, used to seeing the travel agency's carriages come and go, let them through nonchalantly. They were dropped off near the castle; Castle Khaeru, in which a Count Creiz lived.

Count Creiz was an enigmatic man. He'd often sit on the castle floor, appearing to do nothing. The guards wouldn't say anything, fearing reprisal if they spoke up. Other times, he'd speak gibberish to the guards in their faces. They had to stand still and not react; a few times, some guards laughed, and were executed promptly.

He was also a collector of slaves. It wasn't legal under the previous king—King Bastea—'s rule. Now that Ranken was in power, however, the Count could indulge himself in his depraved pastime. His favourite was to try out new women from all over the kingdom, until he found the perfect one. To his dismay, however, none were perfect to his standard. There was always a flaw here or there. Once done with his toy, he'd have them executed, then order a new slave. The turnaround time was a week on average.

About a month ago, his most recent toy arrived. She was almost perfect; almost to his taste, and so, lasted quite a bit longer than usual. Unfortunately, she was just a bit older than perfect, around her late thirties to early forties. *A shame,* thought the Count, *if only I'd found her a few years back.*

—

"Your skin… why?" asked the Count. He was so close this time, but he could see the aging apparent. His newest slave, Mary, had only one flaw—she wasn't in her prime anymore. This was the closest he'd come in years; might be the closest he'd ever get. Should he give up? Maybe stop at this one?

"My lord, what about my skin?" whispered Mary. Her voice was silky smooth, exactly what the Count liked. She had refined it due to the need to keep herself alive.

"You aren't in your prime anymore… huh…" muttered the Count, sighing. He laid back and sunk into his plush bed, pondering. If this was the best he could get, he'd have to stop now. But he wanted the perfect one. No, he *needed* the perfect one. This one would have to go. Making up his mind, he turned to look at his sex slave once more. *You were so close to surviving… whatever your name was. But you aren't there.*

—

Deep underneath Castle Khaeru was a large dungeon. Inside were dozens of men, rebels who had been recently captured. They had sprung up to attack Count Creiz, to seize his land, hoping to stage their assault on Castle Bastea from there. They lost the battle, however, and were now starving to death in the dungeon keep.

"General Junell, here you go. It's all I could get," said the slave. He handed a few bags of food, through the prison bars, to Junell. Junell looked at the slave, nodded, then thanked him.

"Thank you, good sir."

Junell Karisman was the leader of the rebels. He was dark-skinned, native to Southern Terre, bald and brawny. Well, he used to be brawny. Until he ended up in this prison.

It was his idea to take Khaeru; they'd raided towns before, taken over large settlements here and there. But to assault Bastea, you'd need your own castle first. Khaeru was the closest castle to Bastea, so he chose it as their prime target. Unfortunately for him, Count Creiz was no weakling. His forces outmatched Junell's and forced him to surrender. That, or all his men would be executed, as well as all the slaves in Khaeru. Count Creiz was a cruel man who would use any tactic to win. Now Junell and his men rotted away in the dungeon, only hanging on by a thread due to a few slaves who helped them. *They were so brave to risk themselves to help some dead men,* thought Junell. *But in the end, it'll all amount to nothing.*

–

A guard entered the room. Mary was alone, waiting for the summon for her to reconvene with the Count. This time, however, the guard said something different.

"To the courtyard, miss."

Usually the guard would tell her to go to Count Creiz's room. The courtyard wasn't somewhere she went before. Shrugging to herself, Mary got up and followed the guard, unaware of her fate.

—

"Is it morn? Is it night? Is it yesterday or tomorrow? We don't know, we can't know, for we're in the dungeon suffering like a ho!" sang Junell's men.

"Quiet, you lot, some of us are trying to sleep," spoke up a soldier, who was trying to sleep.

"Sleep, sleep for what? Not like we need sleep. We're going to die any day now," clapped back one of the singing soldiers.

"Quiet."

It was Junell who spoke. Instantly, the men became quiet. Junell put his ear to the wall, listening carefully. He had heard some footsteps. Was it the executioner? Or maybe a slave with food? *Let's hope it's food. I'm starving, and so are my men,* thought Junell.

Step...

Step...

THUD.

The person who was walking down the stairs to the dungeon had jumped the remaining set and landed, causing an echo to reverberate around the prison cell. The soldiers looked at each other, unsure of who it was. Junell peeked out of the cell, also trying to ascertain their identity.

"You… I do not recognize you," said Junell. The person was a knight of sorts, wearing unusual armour. He had an unknown insignia on his armour; it wasn't one that Junell recognized. He didn't seem like he was part of Count Creiz's guards, though—he seemed *worse.* He seemed like someone who would be part of King Ranken's inner circle. *Did King Ranken send someone to personally kill me? I guess I'm glad he thought I was that much of a threat to him, at least,* thought Junell.

The knight raised his sword, then slashed downwards at the dungeon lock, cutting it in two. Then, he opened the cell door.

"The rebels of Southern Terre? Consider

yourselves free."

—

Luna climbed on the roof of Castle Khaeru, making sure no one could see her. Lucifer had already entered the castle to see if he could get the rebels out; it was up to her to find Mary. Luna didn't wear heavy armour, making it easier for her to climb, as well as she made much less noise while maneuvering around. They'd got the information from a slave working in the fields by the castle. Well, at least, the information about the captured rebels. Mary was an unknown; it was up to Luna to find out where she was.

Silence… pure silence…

Luna closed her eyes and listened. She heard the wind; laughing, crying, soldiers talking. Her hearing was unlike that of any human's. From this vantage point, she'd hear something, if anything was happening.

The breeze picked up, momentarily cancelling out the noises of the humans. *Breathe in slowly. Breathe out slowly. Focus.*

Then, she picked up something. It was the sound of a guard talking to a female. The guard suddenly had a change in pitch as he talked to a... Count Creiz? Creiz was the leader of Khaeru. Following the sound, Luna crawled towards it. It seemed to be coming from the courtyard.

–

"Stand over there, soldier. And you, slave, on the other side. No, not there. By that pillar," commanded Count Creiz. It was that time again. The time to have fun sucking out the life of a slave, while the guard had to watch. If the guard made any noise, was disgusted at any moment, he would be next. It was fun for Creiz to see both people squirm. He loved the amount of control he had over people —it was pure, adulterous, joyous fun anyone could enjoy.

"Your name... your name? Your name,

what was it again?" asked Creiz. His memory fogged up; too many slaves he'd been through. This one he had forgotten as well. Anne? Jolen? Sara?

"Mary, my lord," answered back the slave.

"Ah, yes, Mary. I remember," he said. He did not remember. "We had a fun time together, wouldn't you say? Lots of fun."

"Yes, my lord. I thoroughly enjoyed it, and you too," replied Mary, her face cheery, her smile radiant.

Creiz frowned. Even now, she seemed so cheerful. Surely she knew what was going to come? *Maybe she's just that dumb,* he thought. *Tch, I like it when they start screaming for mercy better. Whatever.*

"Well, nice knowing your body, uh… Anne? No, Sara… no, Mary… yes, Mary," said Creiz, struggling to remember her name. He then pulled out his sword, levelled it to chest height, then thrust it into Mary's chest.

Even as the life poured out of Mary, she managed to speak. "M-my lord? I always did as you asked…"

"That you did, my dear… Jolen? No… Ma… Maddie? No… Mary? Yes, Mary. Ah, my dear Mary. Unfortunately for you, listening is twenty percent of the equation. The other eighty is looks, and you're a bit older than I'd like," smirked Creiz. Creiz then pulled his sword out of Mary's body and watched as she fell to the floor, clutching her wound, in a desperate attempt to stop the bleeding.

"Oh god—"

The guard quickly interrupted himself, knowing he messed up. The sight of the blood had startled him, and he spoke out loud without thinking. Seeing Creiz turn towards him with a deathly glare, he quickly apologized.

"My lord, I must apologize. I—"

He was cut off by Creiz's sword entering

his mouth, cutting him right through his head. Creiz spat in disgust. Weak guards like him didn't deserve to serve under the great Count Creiz. Now he'd have to find another guard to clean up this mess. There was blood all over the place; it was staining his beautiful marble courtyard red.

—

When Luna arrived, she was too late. She saw Count Creiz stab his own guard, spit on him, then start to stab the guard again. *A weird way of playing with his food,* thought Luna. She focused her gaze on the other victim, the lady. She was on the floor, unmoving, with blood pouring out of her. *Too late...*

Luna jumped down from the roof and landed in the courtyard. Count Creiz looked up to see what it was and saw Luna. She was the most perfect being he had ever gazed upon; it was his perfect lady. In awe, his eyes widened, and his mouth went agape. The goddess had come to him this time.

His answers from God had been heard!

"My goddess, you've finally come to see me—"

Luna thrust her sword into his heart, killing the Count. She retracted her blade, then wiped the blood off on the back part of the coat of the fallen Count. Stepping over his lifeless body, she approached the mortally wounded lady.

"Miss?…" Luna looked at the woman's wound closely. The lady was still breathing, but the wound was fatal. She would die soon.

The lady opened her eyes and noticed Luna looking at her. This wasn't Count Creiz, it was such a pretty girl. What was she doing here?

"Oh, dear, this is a dangerous place… you must…" Mary stopped for a moment to cough. Blood came out of her mouth; she knew she hadn't much time left. She continued, "You must run away from here, it's not safe…"

Luna lifted the woman's chin to get a closer

look at her. She was as Lucifer described; a fair woman, with brown hair and blue eyes. It had to be her. "Is your name Mary Deniere, miss?" asked Luna.

The woman's eyes widened, expressing her shock. Tears came out of her eyes as she replied. "Yes... how do you know?"

"Your son, Lucifer, is looking for you," said Luna. *I don't think he will get to see her alive... unfortunate.*

Mary's voice trembled as she spoke her last words. "Oh, little Lucifer... what a nice friend you've made..."

Luna lay there, not knowing what to do. Lucifer had come all this way to save his mother... yet, at the very end, Mary died. Luna felt sad for Lucifer. Luna herself had never known her own mother, or father, in that accord. She'd always been by herself. But the way Lucifer spoke of his parents indicated they cared for him very much. Just like he took care of her. Luna had never thought she could feel sadness for humans—yet this feeling inside of her, it was definitely sadness.

I'm just a monster... how can I feel this way?

CHAPTER 12

Unified rebellion

Lucifer had already wiped out the guards in the castle. Junell was amazed—a bit scared too—when he saw the carnage around him. There was no way a single person could've done this; yet there was proof right in front of him. This knight was no ordinary man, he was something unnatural. Well, whatever he was, Junell was glad the knight seemed to be on his side. He wouldn't want to ever face him in battle.

"Junell, was it? Secure Khaeru. I have something I must do." The knight's command interrupted Junell from his thoughts.

"Yes, sir. We'll repurpose the weapons

from these dead guards, I guess."

–

Lucifer ran out of the castle, unable to find Luna. Where was she? If he called out, guards might come. He'd cleared the inside of the castle, but the outside still had some patrolling the area, not to mention the rest of the city. But he had no time to spare—it was a risk he was willing to take. Taking in a deep breath, he prepared to yell. *Should I yell for Luna? My mother? Yell something random and hope Luna recognizes my voice?* he thought—

"Lucifer."

Luna jumped down from the roof of the castle, landed beside Lucifer, then embraced him.

"Luna?"

"Count Creiz killed your mother. I was too late to stop him," she finished. Luna slowly turned her head up to look at Lucifer. His face remained emotionless as he stared ahead into nothingness. He wasn't mad at her, was he?

"L-Lucifer, darling, I'm sorry…" whispered Luna. She'd never seen him like this before. He was tense—too tense, and she was afraid of him.

Lucifer lowered his sword and held Luna closer to him. He closed his eyes, but no tears came out. After a while, he finally spoke.

"After we take Khaeru, show me."

—

It was a resounding victory for the rebels. With Lucifer's help, they took back control of Khaeru. Lucifer had rushed around like a madman, slicing up Count Creiz's men with the power of a thousand men. The citizens of Khaeru, who on one hand were glad to finally be free from Count Creiz, were now very scared and concerned about this new knight who had seemingly been able to take control in a day. Junell and his men had to give them reassurances that he was on their side, even though Junell himself wasn't completely at ease. Nevertheless, Khaeru was theirs. Junell would need to thank the knight—as well as attempt to sway him to join him in his fight against King Ranken.

—

"I see. Someone dear to you died here, that's why you came," said Junell. Lucifer stood in front of a freshly dug grave. On the tombstone read the name 'Mary Deniere'.

"I came here to save her. I was too late," whispered Lucifer. He stood stoic, silent. An aura of anger seemed to radiate out from him.

"No, it was my fault, I was too late—"

Luna was cut off by Lucifer. He barked, "Quiet! You are not at fault here."

Luna took a small step back, starting to shake. Lucifer had gone on a rampage throughout the city; after clearing Khaeru of Count Creiz's soldiers, he buried his mother and created her tombstone, carving her name into the stone with his sword. The entire time he had been silent and with that emotionless look on his face. He wasn't like his usual self; he wasn't talking to Luna much. Luna wasn't sure if she was in danger or not as well.

For the first time in what seemed like days, Lucifer's face changed. His expression became one of concern as he realized Luna was scared—scared of him.

"Luna…" he said, walking over to her. "Please don't be afraid of me."

He clutched her close to him, patting her head. He spoke to her gently. "I'm not mad at you. I would never hurt you."

Luna hugged him back, relieved. She should've trusted him, trusted what she knew of him. She had been wrong to think ill of him. *Sadness changes people. He still needs time to grieve.*

Junell cleared his throat, awkwardly watching the drama in front of him. He looked around nervously; no one was nearby. After clearing his throat again, he spoke.

"I supposed this isn't the best time to

talk…" he trailed off.   Lucifer gave Luna a quick kiss, then turned around to face Junell.

"No, now would be fine. What is it that you need?"

"I could surely use someone like you to defeat Ranken. My question is, what will it take to get you on our side?"

"…I believe I'm already on your side."

Junell was surprised at Lucifer's answer. He couldn't believe it at first. "Really? You're after Ranken too?"

Lucifer nodded his head. "Ranken will die by my hands in any case. Helping you on your mission will only make mine easier."

Internally, Junell jumped with glee. On the outside, he appeared calm, as he always did. "Your last name was Deniere, wasn't it? Welcome to the rebellion, *General* Deniere."

–

Junell and his rebels now controlled all of Southern

Terre. A commander of his was leading the charge into Western Terre, and another already making ground in Middle Terre. Learning of Lucifer's escapades in Eastern Terre, he surmised they would receive help from that kingdom when needed. Junell, along with Lucifer, now controlled a decent portion of Terre; with this much control and forces at his disposal, the hopes of a revolution were starting to become true.

"Commander Tengen is fighting to take over Western Terre. Eastern Terre is controlled by King Rakcizs, an ally of yours. We control Southern Terre. Northern Terre is still at war with itself, with Warlords fighting each other for control. Now, we must focus on Middle Terre. General Agenwa, who is leading the vanguard, has already made progress into Polipy. I will assist his efforts there." Junell gestured around the map which was laid out on the table. They were in the war room, near the town of Polipy. Hearing of Count Creiz's fall, many more citizens of Terre had risen up to arms and joined the rebel army. The rebel army had grown in size dramatically, with settlements under Ranken rule falling every day. Some were hard-fought and hard-won, but others fell easily, the people of those settlements siding with the rebels with their joint dislike of King Ranken. Junell then moved his pointer to the city above Polipy, Kanton.

"General Lucifer—if you want, you may take over this city. I will lend you scores of my men if you need."

Lucifer thought for just a second before responding, "No, that won't be necessary. I have my own plan."

Junell was surprised but quickly calmed himself down. "After seeing what you did in Khaeru, I don't think I could sway you otherwise. When me and Agenwa arrive, I'm sure it will already be in your possession."

Lucifer's plan was simple. He would break

in through the front, causing a stir, and kill any guards who resisted on his way to the commander of Kanton, Segundo Seguno. Luna would sneak her way inside, attempt to locate Seguno, and kill him while Lucifer held off the hoards of guards. It relied heavily on Lucifer's inhuman strength; but that strength she didn't doubt, as she'd seen it firsthand many times now.

—

"Hey, Johnny, you feel tired?" asked Len. He had been guarding the gate for a while, but 'twas just another day standing in the hot sun, guarding Commander Seguno. They'd all heard of the recent uprising of rebels and the death of Count Creiz. It seemed like Ranken's 'might equals right' motto of ruling the land wasn't very popular, and perhaps now it was biting him back. It also seemed like one of the rebels was mightier than King Ranken's best warriors. Rumour had it that it was a single knight who had caused the *Carnage at Khaeru*; a giant in terrifying armour who wielded a long, dark-silver longsword. Len didn't believe it, though. Rumours were just that—rumours. It was probably a lot of rebels, and they probably started the rumours themselves. *Yes, that was it,* thought Len. *The rebels are just trying to scare us.*

"Yea, but why? You plannin' on sleeping, Lenny?" retorted Johnny. Johnny sometimes fell asleep while on guard duty, and Len had to always wake him up before the shift changed. If Len were to go to sleep, Johnny would have to stay awake—something he did not enjoy.

"Kind of, you know how you are always sleepin'. I want to sleep for a change, ya know?" replied Len. The sun beamed down intensely. It was a hot day; perfect for an afternoon nap. Sleeping in the shade would feel good, so good…

–

Lucifer entered the main gate without any interference. It appeared that both guards had moved under a tree and were sleeping in its shade. *No matter. Easier for me,* thought Lucifer. He continued towards the inner circle of the encampment, his breath abated, looking for the commander.

–

The mercenary stood over the dead body of his once comrade, who now lay dead on the marble floor of the castle. The mercenary looked up towards the king. He'd won the challenge—now was time for his reward.

"Good, good. You've won. Your name was… Lord Zwein of Rottendoom? Interesting, interesting. Come, come," said Ranken, beckoning towards the mercenary.

Zwein walked over to the king then knelt down in front of him, his hands upturned, waiting for his reward. He felt the soft-felt of a coin purse fall onto his hand. Opening his eyes, he glanced at the sum. Inside the bag contained five gold coins— an amount most would never see in their entire lifetime! Zwein smiled. He had killed eight men to get here; each stronger than the last. It was a tournament held in Castle Bastea, by King Ranken, to see the strongest warrior of the land. The prize in the end was said to be enormous—and it was.

"Oh, and, Lord Zwein. There is one more challenge I have in store for you…" hummed Ranken, smiling. He continued, "A very special challenge, that if you can complete, will net you one hundred gold."

Zwein's head popped up at the mention of one hundred gold. That was an unheard of amount to anyone other than a king! *For that reward. The challenge must be immense,* Zwein thought. *Then again, I have proved that I am the strongest warrior in Terre. There's no one I can't defeat.*

Zwein nodded to the king. He said, "This challenge, tell me about it. I'll complete it easily." He was confident. He was the strongest warrior in the land, as shown by this tournament, after all.

Ranken smiled at Zwein. Finally, he had someone capable enough to take care of the threat in the south. He would have Zwein hunt down the Terror of Khaeru, the one they called Lucifer.

—

"Help! Intrud—"

The guard's words and life were both simultaneously cut short by the appearance of the sword in his neck, which just as quickly as it had appeared, disappeared. The guard's head rolled off his body and tumbled towards the dirt floor, decorating it with red liquid.

The three other guards in the room dropped their weapons and ran, screaming. The Terror of Khaeru had appeared out of nowhere and cleaved a dozen men in an instant—they weren't going to add to that count.

—

"He's here," muttered Zwein. Seguno shifted around nervously, unsure of what was to come. The 'Terror of Khaeru', as he was called, otherwise known as 'Lucifer', was at *his* base. His luck couldn't be more unfortunate. His only consolation was that Lord Zwein had come, sent by King Ranken to assassinate the Terror. But really, what chance did Zwein stand against him? He'd won the tourney at Bastea, sure, but the Terror sure wasn't at the tourney. Sweat dripped down Seguno's forehead, as he would periodically hear the screams of his men outside. They were dying, and quickly. He wouldn't go out there—no way. He had to sit here and lure the Terror inside, where Zwein was strongest. Zwein wielded dual swords, making him more effective in close quarters. Seguno's only chance of survival now was to hope Zwein could beat the Terror.

—

Lucifer ran around the base, searching for Seguno. Periodically, a guard would come, see him, scream, then run away. The base was a mess of a place, adding to the confusion. Lucifer soon realized he was lost in this maze of a base. It was getting dark already; perhaps Seguno had predicted his attack and hid. But where was he hiding?

—

Luna heard Zwein speaking to Seguno. She didn't recognize the voices, but noticed one sounded very calm, the other, panic clearly obvious in his voice. Intrigued and suspicious, she crept up until she saw them through the lock of the door. Indeed, it was the commander of Kanton; alongside him was a heavily armoured soldier wielding twin sabers. *A bodyguard,* she thought, *I may have to fight two-on-one.*

"So... how long do I have to stand here, again?" mumbled Seguno. He had been standing in place for hours now, and his legs hurt.

"Until Lucifer shows up. No sooner, no later. When he comes here, you can scram," replied Zwein.

Suddenly, the door to the enclosed room burst open. A slim figure with a silver longsword stood at the entrance, menacingly. Seguno screamed and ran out through the emergency escape hatch, leaving Zwein behind. Zwein looked ahead, towards the figure, who slowly approached him. *Finally, I meet you, Terror...* Zwein narrowed his eyes as he looked closer. *It's... it's a woman?*

"Impossible!" yelled out Zwein. "Lucifer is a man's name too! You can't be The Terror, I don't believe it. There's no way a broad can be the strongest!"

Luna scowled at the man. Apparently, he had thought she was Lucifer, and now he was assuming she was weak. *Well, I'll show you.*

—

Lucifer stood on top of a tent, scanning the area around. The entire encampment was filled with countless tents, indistinguishable from one another, as they were bought in bulk for a cheaper price. It seemed like Seguno's defensive tactic was to hide. Then, he noticed some movement at the outer wall.

A man was trying to climb over it; he had Ranken's insignia on his chest plate, a commander's helm—Seguno?

Lucifer jumped down and rushed the man. The man turned around, panicked upon seeing Lucifer, then barely managed to climb over the wooden fence. Lucifer drew his sword back and then slashed forward, splintering the fence to pieces, creating a new opening. The man stumbled as he ran, looking backwards in sheer terror at Lucifer. Lucifer charged forward with an ungodly stride and caught up to him in seconds.

"AH! HELPPPP! HELPPPPP!" screamed Seguno. He then tripped on a pebble and fell face-first into the dirt. As Lucifer stopped by him, Seguno closed his eyes and braced for death. This was where he was going to die; in a muddy field outside of Kanton, alone, running away from the enemy.

"Leave," spoke Lucifer, calmly.

Seguno opened his eyes and ever so slightly peered up at Lucifer. He was letting him go? Really?

"R-r-r-really?" stammered out Seguno.

"Yes. Go," repeated Lucifer.

Seguno crawled back up and ran. He ran faster than he ever had before, further than ever before. He was given a chance to live, and by the Devil he'd take it.

—

Zwein looked down in surprise. The battle had only lasted a few seconds; but now, all he could feel was pain. Looking down, there was a sword in his chest, blood gushing out. As Luna pulled out the blade, Zwein stumbled backwards, then landed on the ground with a dull *thud*. Luna licked her blade clean of Zwein's blood before sheathing it.

The tent they were in was of a very similar to the size of her home in the forest; fighting in these close quarters brought back memories of her fighting warlords within those ancient stone walls; her lack of heavy armour a boon, allowing her to outmaneuver her hunters.

As for this fool, you've been beaten by a girl, she thought. Luna walked over to look at Zwein's face, to see his expression before he passed. Zwein's eyes stared forward, at the ceiling, as if not seeing anything.

"Impossible… a woman can't be that strong…" he muttered before he died.

Luna laughed. It was a long, terrifying laugh, a creepy sound a human simply could not produce. The citizens of Kanton heard the cry; they huddled in their homes, afraid to come out. Something devilish had visited their city, and it had wiped out Ranken's troops.

CHAPTER 13

A plot for assassination

Junell's plan was going smoothly. They had made progress in Middle and Western Terre; they already had Eastern and Southern Terre; all they needed now was to stake a claim in Northern Terre. The warlords there had finally solved their land dispute: a single warlord named Lang Langanol had proved his might and killed off all the other warlords. He now ruled Northern Terre. Junell would need to have him removed to complete the first stage of his plan. Lucifer offered to go there, as Gruppen was his home. He had long waited for the time to reclaim Gruppen. The people he knew there were likely still suffering as long as Ranken's men had power.

Lucifer had kissed Luna goodbye a few days ago. He would take back Northern Terre by himself. Luna, on the other hand, had a different task. Her mission was to scout out Bastea castle; look for weak points to attack, see if it was possible to enter the main castle and assassinate Ranken. If they could assassinate him, the rest of the castle would easily fall. Ranken's support had wavered dramatically over the weeks, as the rebels seized more and more control of Terre. Ranken's dominance no longer seemed absolute, and those who followed him from his own philosophy now doubted his might.

—

Luna passed through the main castle walls seamlessly. She had hired the Bastea travel agency, and as a business, they had no worries about a paying customer. They didn't ask her any questions. What they did offer was a luxurious travel experience at a fair price, from Mondays to Fridays.

Once off of the carriage, she made her way towards the main castle. The main castle, where the king's keep was, was a giant, towering building. High up, above the rest of the castle, was a tall, spiralling tower, likely for scouting. On top of its roof were tall spikes which reached up and seemingly touched the sky. Somewhere in the castle sat Dictator–King Ranken. And somewhere up there was an unguarded entrance; Luna would just have to find it.

She scoured the area, keeping note of where the guards were. It had just rained, and the guards nearby were grumbling about the miserable weather. Luna kept her head down as she walked past them. She followed the road, which winded ever closer to the castle courtyard.

One of king Bastea's old guards had given her information about the castle. Deep in the center of Bastea, surrounded by towers, was the castle courtyard. Before the war, it was always green, filled with flowers. The guard didn't know the condition now, but that wasn't why it was important. It was the towers that surrounded it.

The majority of the castle towers were impenetrable from the outside. They had giant spikes protecting the base, making sure no one would be able to crawl up walls there. But the courtyard, protected only by a short wooden wall, had no such spikes. There, one would be able to climb the towers. Of course, being in the center of the towers, it was also one of the most heavily guarded areas.

–

The last light had faded and it was now night; the dreadful rain had come back, pouring down heavily, flooding castle roads. The castle guards started to switch their positions, some retiring to bed, others rotating to new areas. Luna lay hidden behind a bush, nearby the courtyard wall. She'd need only a moment to sneak in. What was on the other side of the courtyard wall, however, she didn't know. She'd have to deal with it then.

The guard leaning on the wall yawned, clearly tired. "Say, Jack, can you handle this by yourself? I'm freezing in this rain. And wet as all hell."

His buddy, hearing this, was not happy.

"What? Lazy bones, you're going to leave me alone again?"

The guard shrugged, knowing his friend would eventually accept. Nothing ever happened anyway. They were in the middle of Castle Bastea too. If anything were to happen, it'd be the gate guards who would be in trouble, not some guards in the center.

"Ah, whatever. Go ahead," relented Jack. At least this time his friend had a valid excuse; usually he just wanted to sleep. He leaned back on the wooden wall and closed his eyes. He was tired, too. A little rest wouldn't hurt.

Luna, seeing her chance, quickly dashed over to a far corner of the wall. The guard made no motion, indicating he didn't see her. Confident she was out of sight, she jumped up and pulled herself over the wall.

She was now in the courtyard of the castle. She quickly looked around; thankfully, it was empty. The grass was still green, as the old guards had described, but quite a few flowers appeared to be dead. The garden of the courtyard had seen better days.

Looking around for a way up, she spotted a wheelbarrow, left out in the rain when the gardening slaves ran for cover. *That'll do.* Luna went on top of the wheelbarrow and used it to climb onto a bush. The bushes on the surrounding edges of the court-yard were tall and sturdy, still trimmed immaculately. She slowly but steadily crawled on top, making her way towards a castle tower.

The tower she decided on had many windows. While using windows might be risky, it was the only way to securely climb up. The other towers were mostly just stone. Unless there were loose bits, it would be very difficult to climb.

It was an old, stony building; aside from the windows, there were a few nooks and crannies for her to obtain purchase on. It was very wet from the rain, though, so she crept upwards carefully. As she went up higher, she felt a bit nauseous. *Don't look down, Luna. Keep going,* she told herself.

Upon climbing to the fourth floor, she looked up and noticed an opening. There was an open window on the fifth floor. There! She'd enter the building through that opening. She had a chance to end the war right now—if she got in. *I can do this.* Raising her arm, she lifted herself up once more, then her foot—

Then her foot felt nothing. She looked down and saw that the tiny brick she stood on had broken off. As her strength waned, she desperately tried to climb down, find another path. But everything was becoming too wet, too slippery in the downpour. She had to get down. It was going to be difficult. One foot at a time. One hand at a time. Left hand; loose brick, but it holds. Right hand—

Her hands slipped, and she fell.

Lucifer, please cry for me.

–

As Lucifer rode into Gruppen, Langanol's men fled. They too had heard of the Terror of Khaeru. The knight that rode into the town definitely fit the description. They didn't want to become part of the next story, likely to be called something like the *Terror of Gruppen*.

If they do not wish to fight, so be it.

The words of his father echoed in his mind constantly throughout the war. He'd spared many men. The ones who ran, who laid their weapons down. Those who cowered when he arrived. There was no reason to slay those who had given up, those without the will. Many were conscripts, too. They weren't there of their own free will; many would rather be on the rebels' side.

Lucifer got off his horse, borrowed from Junell. Junell had given him his fastest horse for the job, knowing the distance to Gruppen. Patting the horse on the back, he then pushed open the gate to Castle Gruppen. Somewhere in here was the warlord Langanol.

–

"What? Fight! FIGHT!" thundered Langanol. He had just received word of Lucifer's entry to Castle Gruppen. The messenger shook as the warlord spoke again.

"TELL EVERYONE TO FIGHT! IT'S LITERALLY ONLY ONE MAN. FIGHT HIM NOW!" screeched Langanol at his messenger.

The messenger trembled as he quickly bowed then ran out the throne room. He had no intentions of telling anyone anything. He was going to get out of Gruppen as fast as he could.

—

As Lucifer entered the castle, the resistance he met was minimal. Langanol's men ran away at the sight of him. The only resistance so far was a door, locked by some guards, but easily cut apart with his sword. The guards behind the door shrieked in fear and spread away from Lucifer like a bunch of cock-roaches suddenly exposed to light.

While he walked through the castle hall-ways, memories of his past flooded him. Cheerful memories of him and his parents, playing in the castle, when times were easy. It was nostalgic but sad at the same time. Nothing could ever be the same again; not when his parents were dead.

He stopped in front of the throne room. The giant, heavy wooden doors were closed tight. Mur-murs of some men could be heard behind the door.

"Another chair, stack another chair."

"A table too. Anything heavy."

"OR YOU COULD FIGHT THEM, THERE'S LITERALLY TEN OF YOU HERE, HOW ARE YOU SO SCARED OF ONE GUY?"

Something strange was happening in there. Lucifer pushed the door, but it only budged a little. Something; multiple things, rather, were behind the door, holding it in place. The voices got noticeably louder when he did so.

"S-someone's trying to enter! Oh Devil almighty, save us."

"What if it's a comrade? They'll die out there!"

"Hell no, if they're out there, let 'em die."

"I AM DISAPPOINTED IN YOU MEN. WHY ARE YOU WHISPERING LIKE COW-ARDS? IF HE CAN HEAR ME IT DOESN'T MATTER ANYWAY."

Lucifer then shoved the doors with a lot more force. This time, the doors flew open, sending chairs and tables flying backwards. The guards, who were behind the stack of rubble, also took flight.

The warlord Langanol could only stare in astonishment at the unreal scene in front of him before he collected himself.

"MEN! HE'S HERE! ATTACK! ATTACK NOW!" he screamed. To his horror, his men did not respond to him. Rather, they split up and started to run away, some even going past Lucifer, out the throne room doors and into the castle grounds.

"W-W-WHY AREN'T YOU ATTACKING THEM? ATTACK THEM, NOT ME!" yelled Langanol to Lucifer. Lucifer seemed to ignore Langanol's escaping men, instead slowly walking towards Langanol.

Then, Lucifer unsheathed his sword, preparing to fight. Langanol, seeing this, raised his axe up. Even if all his men had fled, there was still him. He was the warlord who was able to conquer Northern Terre, after all. He was able to take on anyone before; he'd be able to take out this knight too. His axe raised, he charged forward, screaming.

"YAHHHHHHHHHHHHHHHHHH!"

As Langanol brought his axe down, he expected the power of the blow to make the knight crumple to his knees. Langanol was a huge and burly man, after all. This attack, his overhand charge, would always cause his opponent to fall.

But the knight stood fast, seemingly unfazed by this move. Langanol's eyes went wide as the knight parried the attack, sending him reeling. This knight was stronger than him—how was that possible?

Lucifer levelled his sword and then rushed Langanol before the warlord could recover. Langanol brought his axe down, as fast as he could, to block or deflect the stab.

It wasn't fast enough.

With Langanol dead and his men having run off, Castle Gruppen, and therefore Northern Terre, was finally back in the hands of its rightful ruler.

–

Luna woke up by the bright sunlight that streamed onto her face. When she looked around, she first noticed the metal bars of a prison cell. Then, she noticed how high up she was. There were windows on all sides; all open. Looking out of them, she could see that she was on the tower which was on top of the castle. *So this tower is actually a prison,* she thought, *and if you climb out of the window…* She looked down, and instantly felt vertigo. There was nothing to grab onto for what seemed like an eternity of a distance before there was any semblance of roof to be found. If you climbed out the window, you'd definitely die from the fall.

Then, she heard the shuffling of keys and clank of armour from down below.

Clank…

Clank…

Clank…

It was the sound of two people going up the

tower stairs.

> *Clank...*
> *Clank...*
> *Clank...*

The first person to appear was a guard, who unlocked her prison door. Behind him was a very large, rotund man, dressed in heavy armour. He appeared to be of a high rank; perhaps a commander of King Ranken's.

The large man shoved aside the guard to get a closer look at Luna. He looked at her up and down, seeming to nod in approval.

Then, he opened the prison door and held out his hand, as if expecting her to grab on.

"My name is Sunk Ranken. What is yours, my lovely?"

CHAPTER 14

A demon in distress

"I… I can't believe this…" murmured Sergeant Mackintosh. Lord Lucifer had liberated Gruppen; and now, he wanted Mack to take care of it.

"Mack, you were my father's best friend. You're like my uncle. There is no one else I would rather trust Gruppen to," said Lucifer, looking him in the eye. Mackintosh was straggly and dirty, and looked far from a lord at the moment, but he would serve Gruppen well. He *had* served Gruppen well. He'd only surrendered to save Lucifer and his mother from being executed, after all.

"Do you have to leave? Everyone wants you to stay, my lord," replied Mackintosh. He knew deep down Lucifer would not stay. King Ranken was still out there. But everyone wanted Lucifer to come back, especially as he was now. Lucifer seemed indestructible and capable of anything. He seemed like a god—if gods existed in this mortal world.

Lucifer didn't respond to him; instead, he waved Mackintosh goodbye, and went to find his horse. There was no time to spare.

After killing Langanol, an apparition had appeared before him. Lucifer didn't believe his sight at first; he took off his helmet to rub his eyes, but the apparition was still there. Looking closer, the apparition was wearing a black hooded robe; it drifted across the ground with ease, and it wielded a giant scythe. It appeared as the *Grim Reaper* was described in folklore. But that couldn't be possible. That was only a myth, a fairytale.

Then, it spoke.

"The Demon Maiden has been captured by

King Ranken..."

It hesitated for a second before continuing.

"...forgive my presence. I cannot watch your heart break for the third time."

With that, the grim reaper disappeared. Lucifer still wasn't sure if he was dreaming or not, but he wasn't going to take chances. The reaper told him Luna was in trouble; he'd need to go *now*.

—

"Well, pretty lady, my hand doesn't do? I guess I'll just talk to you for a while, then," smirked Ranken. He took a seat on the prison floor, in front of Luna. She remained silent, motionless. She was disgusted by Ranken. But right now, she could do nothing. Her weapon and armour were nowhere to be seen; probably locked up somewhere deep in the castle.

"So, what brings you to my lovely castle? My guards found you unconscious on the roof o'er the courtyard. That's quite dangerous, climbing the castle. Not very safe now. You could just, you know, ask me to open the door for you, if you wanted to come in," said Ranken. Seeing no reaction from Luna, he frowned. Everyone knew who he was. He was the Dictator–King. She should be trembling in fear, obeying his every command. But she wasn't. Who was she, and what was her deal? Why was she climbing the castle? An enthusiast rock climber, perhaps?

"If you don't want to talk, that's fine as well. I shall come back tomorrow. Perhaps hunger and thirst will coax you to talk, my lovely," said Ranken, ending the visit. He got up with an audible huff, motioned to the guard, then walked down the stairs. The guard locked the prison cell with a loud jingle and followed suit.

A demon can only live so long without water, thought Luna. *How long will I be able to keep silent?*

—

On the second day, Ranken was met with the same

response. The young woman sat there, motionless, completely silent. She stared forward into the void, as if he wasn't there. *She'll crack on the third day. She has to be dying of thirst by now,* he thought. He had a trick up his sleeve though; he wasn't done yet. He snapped his finger; the guard, who had rehearsed the plan earlier, brought him a glass of water. Taking it, Ranken then moved it in front of the girl.

"Just answer my questions, lady, and you can drink as much water as you want. Eat anything you want, too."

Luna kept concentrating on ignoring him. *I can withstand this...* Her body, unhappy with this answer, responded with a growl.

"Your stomach doesn't lie, oh fair maiden. You must be starving..." said Ranken. He motioned to the guard again. This time, the guard pulled out a delicious-looking sandwich. The aroma filled the prison cell, filling it with a delicious scent. "Well? All of this and more. Just talk to me, it's easy."

I... No.

Luna held strong, continuing to ignore him.

Ranken sighed, then took back the food and water. As he thought, it would take a few more days, when she was in serious danger, for her to crack. Yet, he smiled. For her to keep silent this whole time only meant her story was very juicy— something worth the wait.

–

Lucifer's horse was tired. Lucifer wanted to keep going, ride past Renast; but he knew his horse's well-being was important too. The horse would need to be rested to move quickly, after all. So, he stopped at Renast to rest the night. There, at an inn, a soldier recognized him.

"General Lucifer!" called out the soldier. Lucifer looked over his shoulder. It was a rebel soldier, not one that he recognized.

"Hello..." Lucifer responded, unsure of how to respond. What did this soldier want?

"C-Can I have your autograph?" sputtered out the soldier. He held out in front of him his helmet and a pen.

Lucifer frowned. He had become famous; or infamous, depending on which side you were on. This much attention wasn't exactly good, not when it made him a recognizable target for Ranken's army. With a sigh, he took the pen from the giddy soldier and signed the helmet with it. After handing the items back to the soldier, he asked him a question.

"Soldier, where are you headed towards?" Lucifer had a hunch on where the soldier was going. Troops were all convening to Junell, preparing to reinforce Castle Cardela.

"General Junell had requested everyone to join him in Cardela, near Psuert, sir!" said the soldier, enthusiastically.

Lucifer nodded before responding, "Ah, as I thought. Tell him to immediately march for Castle

Bastea when you get there. Obviously, he won't believe you. So say the words 'Lady Luna'. He will understand you then."

"Yes sir! I will not let you down sir!" yelled the soldier. The other people in the inn turned around, noticing his loud voice. Blushing, the soldier walked back to his group of friends, who were astonished. Their friend was given a task by General Lucifer himself. And it seemed like a very important one, at that!

–

As the footsteps grew ever nearer, Luna knew what was to come. She was hungry, thirsty, tired, you name it. She could smell the scent of freshly cooked stir fry already, ever getting closer in sync with the steps. And there they were: the guard and the dictator–king, ready for what, the fourth, fifth, interrogation?

"Ah, do you smell that?" said Ranken, while opening the prison door. "Freshly cooked stir fry. Delicious, if I might say so myself. I'm a nice guy, personally, so I'll let you have it first." He laid down the plate of stir fry in front of Luna, along with a glass of cold water. "Please, enjoy it whenever you're ready."

Luna's mind fought against her body. Her mind told her not to, but her body refused, seemingly forcing her to move. Her hand moved ever so slightly; this motion did not go unnoticed by Ranken.

"Yes, yes, my lovely. Eat up, for you will die of starvation otherwise," he said, with a feigned tone of concern in his voice. He stared at her, intently, watching her every move.

I... I'm so hungry... My throat hurts... I'm so thirsty... Luna struggled to resist, but she couldn't. Her body needed nutrients now. It must have them, or else she would die.

In a second, Luna took off her mask, then swallowed the stir fry in a flash. Then, she gulped down the water in an instant. It all happened so fast, the guard didn't even see what happened.

But Ranken, who was watching her every move, saw it. He saw her shark-like teeth, her unnatural mouth. He instantly knew what she was—she was a succubus.

A large grin overcame him. A fabled demon; one of legends, in his grasp. And she was as beautiful as the legends said. *Thank you, lord Satan,* thought Ranken. *What a wonderful gift you've given me!*

—

"General Junell, one of the reinforcements desperately wants to talk to you," relayed a messenger, who had just run into the war tent. Junell looked up from his desk; he was busy formulating a siege plan to take both Rottendoom and Castle Yvyerst. A regular soldier? Why would they need to talk to the general?

"Well, I'm sure you know they can talk to a

commander instead. I'm busy, if you hadn't noticed," respond Junell, a bit peeved. He was almost done with his plan, too.

The messenger shifted his feet, uncomfortable. The soldier had said this was of utmost importance; that it was a message from General Lucifer. But he wasn't sure if he believed it himself.

"General Junell, the soldier said it was from General Lucifer. That it was incredibly important that you got the message."

Junell scowled. This had to be a joke. But in the slightest chance that it was real, it would be very important. "Bring him in, then. If it's any funny business…" Junell trailed off, sure the messenger got the hint. The messenger nodded, then rushed out of the tent.

Now, should he go for Rottendoom first, or Yvyerst—

A soldier barged into the tent, followed swiftly by the messenger.

"The soldier is here to relay the message, sir!" shouted out the messenger, breathing heavily now.

Junell waved his hand, giving the soldier permission to speak. The soldier could scarcely contain himself.

"I met General Lucifer at Renast! H-he signed my helmet, see!"

The soldier pointed to his helmet, where there was indeed the signature of Lucifer. But a skilled writer could forge a copy. This didn't mean anything to Junell.

"Message, now."

Junell glared at the soldier, who seemed to be wasting his time. He didn't care if he got an autograph or not. That wasn't important.

"Ah, yes, uh… yes! General Lucifer wants you to march on Castle Bastea… like immediately!" shouted out the soldier. He looked at Junell nervously, whose scowl was growing angrier as he heard more words coming out of the soldier's mouth. As if Lucifer would simply just decide to attack Castle Bastea on a whim! That was their final target; they were a ways off. They still had to secure Western Terre and Middle Terre before they could ever *dream* of facing off Ranken.

"Out. OUT!" yelled Junell. This had been a colossal waste of time. This soldier did all this for what, fame? Clout? He'd be in prison for a week instead, to think about the stupidity he'd just subjected the general to.

The soldier's mouth went agape in shock as guards started to pull him out. He did meet General Lucifer though. He was told the message! The code words... the *code words*!

"Lady Luna!" he screamed out, trying to resist the guards.

Junell froze. Only the high command even knew Luna existed, though most just considered her as General Lucifer's maiden. The only people who knew her name were Junell… and Lucifer. This could only mean one thing. Lucifer somehow knew Luna failed her mission. How, he did not know. What Junell did know was that he had to assemble his army quickly. General Lucifer, as strong as he was, was only a single man. He stood no chance against King Ranken's army alone.

I'll save you, friend. Don't you die on me!

–

Lucifer waited outside Castle Bastea, scouting the area out. There was no way he would be able to get in normally; he was too recognizable now. Everyone recognized him; they either treated him as a hero, or a monster to run away from. He would only be able to enter the castle by using force. But that would mean fighting thousands of soldiers to get to the main castle—something completely unthinkable. Lucifer beat himself up internally—Luna was in there and he couldn't do anything. He was so strong, but at the same time, so weak. At that moment, he felt powerless; useless. *If I can't protect the one person I love the most… can I even call myself strong?*

The horn was loud and clear. Right after it, came the thunder of thousands of hooves racing across the ground. Lucifer looked around until he spotted it—it was the coalition army, thousands strong, in the distance.

You did it, soldier.

The rescue of Luna had begun.

CHAPTER 15

All in

There was a chained collar attached to Luna's neck. It had just been fitted on when she heard the shouts of worried guards, calling out the sight from across the castle walls.

"The rebels are attacking—along with the massive army of Eastern Terre!"

"I-I see the flag of Northern Terre as well!"

"What happened to that Warlord Langanol? Thought he took control there..."

"There's fucking thousands of them. To your stations, RIGHT NOW!"

Ranken, hearing the cries of his men panicking, scowled and rushed out to a window to see.

In front of the castle, *his* castle, was the giant coalition army. Siege towers from Eastern Terre, the cavalry of Southern Terre; they were far in the distance, but coming closer by the second.

"Damn it all! Kill them! Kill all those scum!" yelled out Ranken. Ranken then collapsed to the floor, defeated. He knew this day would come. His lords were being killed left and right; the kingdom's support for him dying down. It was inevitable. But this soon? It made no sense. If he had his entire army here, he'd easily win. But they were split up, a large portion on a mission to defend Western Terre. It just wasn't fair!

There was still a good chance his army could win, though. They were defending, and Castle Bastea's walls were nigh impenetrable. He'd know. He had to go past them to kill king Bastea, after all. Unless they broke through the main walls, he shouldn't be worried. Yes, just send a messenger to Rottendoom, and Commander Dreid's army would arrive in two days. Castle Bastea would easily hold out that long. He didn't have any reason to worry, after all.

Then he noticed the succubus staring daggers at him. He had almost forgotten about her, whilst deep in his thoughts. A grin slowly made its way to his face. Instead of worrying about the siege, he would have some fun. *Oh jolly, what fun! Satan, glory thee!*

–

Lucifer ran up the stone wall, *vertically;* it was a good fifty or so meters to the top of the wall, but he somehow made it—as if he had an invisible wing lifting him up. The archers on the wall, surprised, confused, and perhaps frightened by the sight, ran screaming and scattered away quickly. The few that chose to draw their shortswords and fight lasted a whole of two seconds before becoming part of the environment. Lucifer jumped down from the wall, smashing a cloud of dust when he landed, then ran towards the main castle.

"T-The Terror! Stop h—"

The soldier's cry was cut short by his lack of vocal cords, which had suddenly disappeared along with his head. Lucifer charged onward, killing the men in his path who dared to raise their swords at him. Most, however, fled the area. The rumours were true—the Terror Knight was just as monstrous as legends claimed, and he was heading straight for the center of the castle. Let him have the castle; inner Bastea, Ranken. The conscripts wanted no part in the massacre.

—

Ranken brushed Luna's dark hair to the side, exposing her entire face. She was beautiful; it was unreal. *This is the beauty of a succubus,* thought Ranken. *A human could never be this appealing.* He took a closer look at her mouth; it was kind of disgusting to look at, sure, but as long as she had the mask on, it was fine. The rest of her was absolute perfection. He would enjoy having his way with her.

Ranken laid his golden axe to the side, then began taking off his clothes. Without anyone to help him, though, he struggled at first, the clothing that once fit him well now stretched to their limits from his newfound weight gain. After grunting for a while, he was finally able to remove a single shirt.

Luna looked around the room. It was a giant room—the king's room, once old king Renald Bastea's. She was chained by the neck to the bed; there was no way to escape. Wait a moment—there, in a chest in the corner. Something silver stuck out of it, something familiar. Her sword! Her shoulder and hip armour must be in there, too. If she could somehow manage to get it, she'd be able to escape. But she needed to escape to get her weapon… Perhaps this was her fate.

Ranken was now naked. His member, which had already been erect, instantly popped out of his pants when he took them out, though it was barely visible underneath his long, filthy pubic hair. He stroked it a few times, moaning, while staring at Luna. Now it was her turn to take off her clothing. He motioned to her, expecting her to understand. Luna sat still, refusing. *Fine,* he thought, *I'll have to undress you myself.*

He climbed onto the giant bed beside Luna, and started to lift up her crop top. Luna opened her mouth and bit his arm, hard. Ranken yelped, grimacing in pain. The succubus' razor-sharp teeth had cut deep into his right arm, causing it to bleed profusely.

"You whore, you'll pay for that!" shrieked Ranken. Just as he was about to jump on Luna, to smother her, perhaps, his bodyguard flung open the door.

"King Ranken! The Terror Knight is inside the castle! We must escape, now!"

Ranken turned, in horror. The Terror, inside? How was that possible?

The bodyguard, seeing Ranken's indecision, pressed again. "Sir, we MUST hide now! He's already in the castle!"

Ranken, finally comprehending the danger he was in, rushed to gather his clothes. His mind was now fully fixated on escaping the Terror; the succubus, he'd leave for the Terror to kill. Unfortunate, though, as he never got to have fun with her. And who knew if he'd ever find another succubus out in the world. *Drat, damn it! But if the Terror kills her cleanly,* thought Ranken, *maybe enough of her body will still be there to play with...*

–

Lucifer smashed through the king's bedroom window, shattering the glass to hundreds of pieces. There sat Luna, chained to the bed, weeping softly. Lucifer rushed over, then cut off her collar carefully. She leapt up and embraced him.

"You came just in time, darling."

Lucifer gave her a quick kiss before separating himself from her embrace. They didn't have much time.

"Hurry, we must go before the ruse is up."

Luna nodded, then ran to the chest in the corner. She opened it up; as she had surmised, inside were her armour and sword. Lucifer came over and helped her put her armour back on. Once finished, he motioned for her to get on his back. She obliged—but she did not expect him to jump out the window.

—

Junell held his hand up, bringing the army to a halt. This was the failsafe Lucifer had planned. In case anything happened to Luna, they'd send their strike force to appear to attack Castle Bastea, causing pandemonium inside. Lucifer would then enter the castle during this time and rescue Luna as the soldiers were distracted. Junell could only hope Lucifer had succeeded. The army would have to pull back before they got into actual fighting range; they weren't strong enough, not now.

"Sir, what's going on?" asked a commander, confused. All he knew was that they were doing a hail-mary attack on Castle Bastea, while Ranken's forces were reinforcing Rottendoom. For Junell to stop the momentum seemed off.

Junell responded curtly. "Call off the attack. Everyone retreat to Cardela. We shall prepare for the invasions of Rottendoom and Yvyerst once again."

The commander, while confused, did not question his general. He nodded, then ran back to give the news to the army.

–

Arrows hit the ground where Lucifer and Luna were moments before as they escaped the castle on horseback. Soon, the sounds of whizzing arrows faded away. They were out of the danger zone.

Luna had held onto Lucifer for dear life as he sprinted down the castle roads at breakneck speeds. He moved faster than his steed could, his strides covering dozens of meters at a time. Soldiers in their way had to get out of the way lest they end up flattened.   Lucifer then ran *up* the main walls, vertically, then jumped off. Luna couldn't believe her eyes at the moment; even now, it seemed like it was a dream.

The events of the day had tired her out. *Maybe this was a dream.* She started to doze off, the regular thumping of hooves on the ground becoming background noise.

"Luna."

Her eyes fluttered open, and the sound of hooves jolted her back to reality. She lifted her head up. Lucifer had his head turned; he was looking at her.

"Luna? Are you okay?"

"I—yes," said Luna. Should she tell him what happened? Maybe later. It was too traumatizing to recall, at the moment. She shuddered at the thought of Ranken. She didn't want to remember that at all. All because she fell from the tower; she didn't even make it inside. She failed her mission…

But how did Lucifer know she was in trouble? He had to have been in Gruppen when she was imprisoned. She shook her head. *Nevermind that.* What mattered was she was safe again.

—

Ranken and his guards had run deep underground of the castle. So far, in fact, that they were lost. They had never seen this part of the castle; it was completely dark, damp, and terrifying. The guard in front, who carried a lantern, was visibly shaking. The others behind him kept prodding him, making sure he'd keep moving forward.

Drip…

Drip…

Drip…

Water fell from somewhere in the distance. Ranken shivered; it was getting cold. It was wet. It was dark. He didn't like this. But none of his guards knew where they were, and he had no choice but to follow the guard in front, the one with the light.

Drip...

Drip...

Drip!

The sound of the water was getting louder. That meant they were close to... *something.* As the group shuffled along, the air started to get more musty and thick, smelling of soot. An aura of something unnatural filled the area, causing a guard to scream and leave the group. In only a moment, he disappeared into the darkness. The others now huddled together, too afraid to move.

"Bah! Cowards, all of you! Gimme the light!" shouted Ranken, pissed. He grabbed the lantern from the frontal guard and lifted it up. Then, he walked towards the sound of water.

Drip...

DRIP....

DRIP!

There, in front of him, was a large, circular *thing,* ever so slightly glowing. Inside the glowing circle was pure darkness. The light from the lantern was unable to reflect off of whatever it was. The musty, sooty smell, faint at first, was now over-powering. The sound of water came from the stone roof, falling regularly, onto the ground. It pooled into a small stream that flowed into the circular thing, disappearing inside it.

The guards, now convinced this was super-natural, went on their knees and started to pray. Ranken, a firm believer in Satan, saw this as some-thing else. Something *holy.* Whatever it was, it must've been created by Satan, for his stoutest fol-lowers. Perhaps the biggest worshipper of the Devil, Ranken saw this as a gift. He took a step into the hole and disappeared.

The guards, seeing this, froze in fear. Their king was one moment there—the next, gone. Into the hole. They stared at the hole for what seemed to be an eternity, waiting for Ranken to appear. When he didn't, they slowly turned to each other, screamed, then ran off. In what direction, no one knows.

—

Commander Dreid looked into his binoculars for what may have been the hundredth time, waiting for the attack. But there were no forces in the distance. It was getting dark by now; the scouts had predicted an attack by noon. They were wrong.

A guard stood by, nervously. His commander had been walking in circles the entire day, waiting for the attack. Something had to be wrong; the scouts wouldn't have false information. They were always accurate. He had been standing there all day, too, because he had to guard Dreid. But his legs were starting to go numb, and he wasn't sure how much longer he could keep standing still.

Footsteps came; they belonged to a messenger.

Commander Dreid snapped his attention to the man. He was ragged, dead tired; he had run through two horses to get there in a day. Whatever message he had must've been important.

"Huff, huff…" panted the messenger, who struggled to catch his breath. "Ra… Dictator–King Ranken requests reinforcements at the castle. It's under siege…"

So that was where they were. It was all a ruse; to get them to reinforce Yvyerst and Rotten-doom, while they struck Bastea? Smart play. Commander Dreid finally stepped off the watchtower, then sprinted towards the barracks. Duty called, and it was time to defend Castle Bastea.

CHAPTER 16

Hell

The first thing Ranken noticed was the sky. It was dark red; there was no sun, yet red light rays some-how managed to stream through the black clouds. Looking closer at the ground, he then noticed the valley deep beneath him was filled with lava. In it were tiny dots; of what, he couldn't make out of it.

He stood on a small rock ledge, suspended from the valley by a few hundred meters. Attached to the platform was a rocky bridge that seemed to go on for kilometers. Turning around, there was noth-ing. No sign of the portal he'd used to enter. Shrugging to himself, there was only one way to go. Forward.

He walked for what seemed like hours when the first sign of life appeared. The rock bridge finally widened, turning into a vast platform. There were streetlights at the end of the bridge; reddish-orange in colour, swaying slowly, back and forth, from the winds of this world.

There, by the lights, appeared a stone road. Like the bridge, there was only one path—forward. Grunting in exertion, Ranken pushed on ahead; his body tired, but his mind excited. This was the world described as hell. This was where his god, Satan, lived!

—

The town started out small, with only a few people wandering about. The buildings were made of dark stone and wood. The main road was brightly lit up and decorated with silk streamers and floating lanterns. There was a festival of sorts going on.

The people were peculiar. They were dressed in bright colours; for the occasion at hand.

They were mostly around the same age; none were too old, nor too young. *Odd,* thought Ranken, *this is kinda creepy.*

As Ranken walked past them, his exhaustion from the long walk grew. He needed to find a resting spot, or meet Satan quickly. Looking about, he spotted a middle-aged woman, sitting on a bench, by herself. *A good candidate,* he thought. *She'll know something.*

"Ahem... uh, excuse me," snorted Ranken, trying his best to be polite. He didn't know how the citizens of hell would react if he acted like his normal self. They were dead, right? He didn't want to incur their wrath, lest he end up dead, too.

The woman raised her head, eyeing him suspiciously. "Personally, I would've reincarnated in my best shape, but that's just me. Personally. Um, what do you want?"

Ranken scowled, not sure what she meant. *Probably some dead people mumbo jumbo,* he thought.

"Satan... you know Satan, the Devil?"

The woman nodded her head. Ranken, excited to hear this, continued.

"Ah, you know where I can find him?"

The woman turned her head to the left, looking into the distance. Then, she pointed towards where she was looking. "Just keep following the road. Lord Satan's castle is massive. You can't miss it once you're there."

Ranken mumbled a 'thank you' and then proceeded on his journey. He'd meet his maker, at last! He couldn't wait to meet him; surely Satan knew of his exploits on Terre. That he'd brought his name to the forefront of religion. As his biggest worshipper, he'd surely get a king's welcome.

—

The building was indeed massive. Lengthwise, it appeared unending, stretching off into the distance. Heightwise, it stood a hundred meters tall, with hundreds of windows to boot. It was a huge, grey wall of power. At the bottom lay the road to the building. Dotted alongside it regularly were guards; huge, frightening, and dressed head to toe in black armour.

Ranken nervously shuffled up the road, aware of his peril, but the guards stood still, motionless. Seeing no action from them, his confidence grew; he started to walk faster, getting closer to the entrance, bit by bit.

The entrance doors were already open. In front of Ranken was a person, dressed in all white, who held a large parcel in his hands. Ranken, unsure of where to go from here, decided to follow them.

The building's halls were tall and haunting. It was dark in here; a few flames lit up the ceiling, but not enough to remove all the shadows present. Multiple entranceways were accessible from the main hall, adorned with grey arches finished with a metallic sheen.

The person shuffled towards the right side

of the building, into one of the entranceways. Ranken, following behind, took each step tentatively. Each step, however, caused echoes to bounce off the large walls, producing an eerie sound. The person in white, however, seemed not to notice, continuing their journey.

They reached a small door. The person in white pushed it open, revealing a spiralling staircase behind. They held the door open; Ranken, surprised, walked through.

The two slowly climbed the seemingly never-ending staircase. They passed by many other doors, but did not stop. It was only at the top did the person in white open the final door.

The final door, at the end of the staircase, led to the top floor. The floor was vast; it was just a large, empty hall, only adorned by giant windows on the southern side. On the floor was a long, giant carpet. At its end were another set of doors; these one massive in size, stretching from the ground to the ceiling.

The person in white walked on the carpet, heading towards the large doors. Ranken, who had been peering out the windows and enjoying the view, quickly went back in line and followed. This area seemed important; Satan had to be in here!

–

The person in white went in first. Ranken stood back, at the doors, watching. He had no clue what to do; observing what the person did would be a great boon for him.

Ahead, in the center of the massive room, sat a man on a throne. He wore red robes and a red hood. Around him, one behind each shoulder, were two beautiful women, each fanning him with a large leaf. The man on the throne, noticing a visitor, put down the bowl of grapes he was eating.

"My lord, on this day, the holy day of salvation. I offer to you my most precious of gifts," spoke the person in white. He knelt down, arms outstretched, offering the parcel.

Satan mused a bit, stroking his beard. This citizen was quite late. The majority of gifts had already been offered earlier in the day. Well, better late than never. He grabbed the boxy parcel then opened it. Inside were grapes; the finest in all the underworld, straight from the vineyard.

Satan sighed. This was probably the hundredth time someone offered grapes. He liked them, sure, but he already had too many. Rolling his eyes, he then turned his attention back to his subject.

Their head remained down; their body trembling in anxiety.

"Fine, whatever, it's fine. You may leave."

The subject stood up, relieved. He nodded his thanks and swiftly left. The next person in line was a rather rotund man. Satan gazed at him; he'd never seen this person before. He motioned to the man with his hand, beckoning him to come. The man nervously shuffled forward, then kneeled down and bowed to him.

"Oh, my lord, dost thou recognize me…?" asked Ranken, excited. His exploits in the overworld had to have been noticed by Satan, right?

Satan frowned, not sure what this guy was talking about. He'd never seen him before.

"No, who the fuck are you?"

Ranken's eyes went wide in surprise. His voice trembling now, he responded.

"Uh… my lord, I am Dictator–King Ranken of Terre… the one who killed King Bastea?"

Satan's stare remained blank, showing that he had no clue what Ranken was talking about. Ranken, recognizing the silence as confusion, continued.

"The leader of the reformed Devil's Cult… me? Sunk Ranken? Ruler of Terre?"

Satan scoured his mind, thinking of the words he'd just heard. He recognized them from something. *Terre… ah, yes, the overworld,* he thought, *I hadn't seen that shit in how many years?*

"You're here... meaning you died, so not the ruler anymore," snickered Satan. He continued. "Anyway, where's my present?"

Ranken looked left, then right, thinking he might've been talking to someone else. When he realized that he was the only patron in the room, he looked back up at Satan, who seemed a tad bit disappointed.

"Uh... uh, I am your most loyal follower on Terre, l-lord. I-I ruled all of Terre, set you as the new god, don't you care?" said Ranken, stammering. He was shaking in fear now; Satan, for some reason, didn't seem to understand.

"Listen..." said Satan, now standing up.

"I don't give no fucks about Terre. I don't give no fucks about the ruler. I haven't given any fucks for a thousand years. WHERE THE FUCK IS MY PRESENT?"

Satan screamed it out, veins bulging. His

face was now visibly red; the two women behind him had stopped fanning, now in shock.

Ranken froze in fear, not sure what to say. He had to get his message across—Satan had to understand!

"M-my lord, I rule Terre, I am your most devout—"

A bright light flashed; a great cleaver sword appeared, directly in Satan's right hand. He swung down, cleaving the ruler of Terre in two. As Ranken's body started to separate, Satan sat back down. He had had enough of the fool's ramblings. A servant nearby, noticing the mess, rushed forward to clean up Ranken's remains. It wasn't the first time he'd witnessed this, and it certainly wouldn't be the last.

—

Commander Dreid had been awake for two days. His army rode like the wind, for Dictator-King Ranken needed their help. A siege on Castle Bastea was foolish; it was foolish of Junell to think he could prematurely end the war here and now.

"The castle—it's fine!"

"I don't see any fighting."

"Quiet, quiet!" shouted out Dreid. His men, seeing the castle, had started to chatter amongst themselves. Hearing their commander, the men's voices died down.

"All seems well—but do not keep your guard down. It could be a surprise, a ruse," stated Dreid. It was very unlikely, but he wouldn't take the chance. His men nodded in agreement, then continued marching forwards. Soon, they'd find out whether or not the castle was theirs or not.

–

The castle was in disarray. King Ranken had gone missing, as had most of his personal bodyguards; all but one. The current commander in charge, Commander Wisle, was indecisive. He didn't know what to do now that Ranken was gone.

"You, Wisle! Where's Ranken?" yelled out Dried.

"Er, I dunno. He must've ran away some-where..." shrugged Wisle, unsure. "I mean, one of 'is guards is back, but he's gone loony, see."

"*Loony?* What? Show me."

—

The guard was in prison. He'd been locked up after returning from that horrific basement, mumbling nonsense. Even then, sitting in his cell, he remained crazed, talking about a deep basement that didn't exist. The prison guards didn't like it one bit.

"That man's off his rockers, ain't he,"

"Left Ranken fer dead somewhere, prob-ably. Belongs in the prison, he does."

Then came loud footsteps, followed by voices, coming down the prison. The prison guards immediately stopped chatting, adjusted their pos-ture, and stood still.

"...he's been mumbling crazy talk, see.

Look, that 'un o'er yonder. Talk to 'im and you'll see," said Wisle, pointing to the cell. Dreid narrowed his eyes, struggling to see in the dimly lit prison area. Yes, there he was. A man sat on the prison floor, hunched over, talking to himself. Wisle and Dreid walked over; the rantings became louder. Now, Dreid could hear some of what the man was talking about.

"Dictator-King Ranken, why must we go?"

"The Terror is here, we must run…"

"No light, water… no light, water!"

Clank.

The man froze, hearing someone bang on the prison bars. He turned to look, and saw a few men staring at him. The badges on them were familiar—yes, he recognized them. They were commanders.

"You there, the only guard remaining of King Ranken's. Where is he?" questioned Dreid. *Something must have really gone wrong for this to happen,* he thought, *something bad.*

"Yes, we went into the basement, yes. Large hole in wall, yes… darkness… all darkness… sound of water, drip, drip, drip…"

Wisle rolled his eyes up, exasperated.

"That's about all you'll get outta 'im, now. He just repeats himself, o'er and o'er again, see."

With a huff, Dreid left the prison. The others followed him, glad to be away from the dark area. As he walked up the stairs, a grin started to form on his face. With Ranken gone, no one would be able to stop him from taking control. He'd be the next ruler of Terre!

CHAPTER 17

An accidental plan

The Rottendoom guard stretched his legs, tired. He had been sitting on the watchtower all day and desired rest. He looked around him; barely any other guards were there. No one would notice; no one would care. With Commander Dreid headed to Bastea, his army with him, Rottendoom was peaceful. No one really was in charge here. The guard, making one last attempt to clear the area, decided now was the time. He knelt down, then lay on the floor. It was time to sleep.

> *Whizz...*
> *Whizz...*
> *Thunk!*

The guard woke up, startled. What he had just heard sounded like an arrow smashing into wood. He wiped his eyes, still groggy, then stood up.

Thoom.

The arrow went into his head, killing him instantly. In the distance, the thunder of cavalry began to grow louder. The capture of Castle Rotten-doom had begun.

–

"Close the gates! Close the gates!" screamed a sol-dier in the distance. They had been surprise attacked; at the worst moment too. Their forces had been split up; the Yvyerst army, commanded by Dreid, headed towards Bastea and had the vast majority of soldiers. Rottendoom, on the other hand, had only a small army; thinking the entire enemy force was at Bastea, the Rottendoomers were unpre-pared for the surprise attack; many were still barely awake, struggling to get out of the barracks.

"On the ramparts, go, go, go!"

"An arrow's in my knee, my knee!"

"AHH—"

More screams littered the castle yards, the owners of which soon became silent, a result of the terrifying cloud of arrows that rained down upon them.

The Lieutenant of Rottendoom, Lieutenant Jones, ran into the barracks, wondering why only a few soldiers had come out. There stood hundreds of men, still sat on their beds, too afraid to join the battle.

"MOVE. FUCKING COWARDS," shrieked Jones. He ran past soldiers, flailing at them with his arms. "MOVE!"

The soldiers trembled, still too afraid to do anything. Seeing this inaction enraged Jones. He drew his sword and aimed it at the closest soldier, a young man who had just been drafted.

"You. MOVE! NOW!"

The soldier froze in fear, unable to do anything. Jones, after waiting a second, had enough. He slashed at the soldier, giving him a fatal wound. As the soldier gurgled out blood, Jones turned to the rest of the soldiers, whose eyes were wide from what they'd just seen. "IF YOU DON'T MOVE, I'LL KILL YOU MYSELF. MOVEEEEE!"

–

Inside the large walls of Rottendoom was the city itself; the buildings were blocky and squarish in construction. Its street, regular and orderly, would normally be filled with citizens going about their daily lives. Right now, however, it was littered with the bodies of dead soldiers.

Lucifer ran down the main road, heading directly for the inner castle. The few soldiers who drew their weapons at him were quickly executed; they were but another pebble on the ground to him. Others, witnessing the horrific scenes with their own eyes, dropped their weapons and ran.

The tallest tower, that must be it.

Lucifer jumped up, landing on the wall, then sprinted upwards, carried by his momentum. Once on the fourth floor, he struck a window with his metal gauntlet, sending shards of glass flying everywhere. He hoisted himself up and through the window pane, rolling into the room it had once protected.

It was a simple hallway, spanning south to north. Lucifer took a moment to catch his breath, and also to listen to the sounds of panic that echoed through the walls.

"...cowards, the lot, you too! MOVE!"

The voices came from the north side. Lucifer snuck his way towards the sound.

"MOVE! MOVE! MOVE! You, MOVE! Cook? Don't care, MOVE, NOW!"

The main voice, who was shouting orders, belonged to an old male's. *Probably the leader,* Lucifer thought, based on the way he was treating everyone around him.

—

Commander Jones glared at the last staff member, a cook, who had cowered underneath a chopping table. The cook, fearful for his life, ran away. Jones sighed in frustration. He still had a few more floors to clear. He'd need everyone he could muster to hold off the invading army. But for now, he was exhausted from his yelling. He needed a short break; a pint of beer would suffice. Then, he heard a creak from behind him.

"What did I tell you—"

Jones stopped himself, mid-sentence, as he now saw who opened the emergency door. It was a tall knight, dressed in black armour, holding a long, dark-silver sword. It matched the description of the Terror. *The Terror Knight!*

Lucifer rushed forward, blade drawn horizontally. The commander didn't have a chance to react; the top half of him was already sliding off as

Lucifer flicked his blade clean, attempting to remove the blood from it. Lucifer looked at the insignia the man wore—it was that of a lieutenant. This was likely the current leader of Rottendoom. Now, time to make the troops surrender.

—

When Lucifer ran out of the tower, the streets were already cleared. The battle had already been won; the defending troops, being severely outmatched, gave up quickly. The conscripts, making up the vast majority of the army, were unwilling to die for the cause of the Devil. Others—the mercenaries, the believers—seeing the carnage, had run away from Rottendoom, not eager to join the fate of their dead comrades.

Now Lucifer had to find Luna; make sure she was safe. She told him she'd be fine. To trust her. Even so, he couldn't help but be afraid for her safety. The events at Bastea still haunted his mind; when she told him what Ranken tried to do to her, he had become furious.

"Lucifer, Lucifer!"

The sweet melody belonged to Luna. She had spotted Lucifer running down the street. Lucifer, seeing her, rushed over to give her an embrace. He held her body in his arms, not wanting to let go. Her hair smelled of roses; her sparkly green eyes twinkled in pleasure.

"I'm fine, I'm fine!" she stated. Lucifer let go of his hug, staring into her, eyes still filled with concern. He had been constantly hovering over her lately, ever since the rescue. He then hugged her again, drowning her body in his arms.

"Good."

–

"Soldiers of the coalition. Hear me now—we are but one step to victory!" shouted Junell. The crowds of men and women beneath him cheered, ecstatic. They'd swept through Rottendoom and Yvyerst easily. The four main regions of Terre now lay in rebellion control. A few cities, like Rotodyn and Zundan, remained under Ranken's control, but the local lords would soon take care of that. All that remained for the main army was to finally lay siege on Castle Bastea—for real, this time.

"My brother, General Agenwa Karisman, will lead his southern cavalry. Commander Tehla Tengen will lead his curved blades in a surprise attack from the west. King Rakcizs will command his siege towers from the east. And I shall lead the main troops from the north. Everyone, the next time we meet, shall be in Bastea!"

The crowd roared in approval. Finally, after years of bloodshed. They'd finally be able to take back their land. This time, remove the Devil's cult for good.

Up high, on the wooden stage, Junell shook his head, weary from his speech. Lucifer, standing in a dark corner with Luna, glanced at the general. He'd been leading the army since day one, nonstop.

Was he tired?

Junell, noticing his friend, relayed his thoughts.

"That speech wasn't my best. I don't know how I sounded to the troops, you know?"

Lucifer shrugged, unworried, then said, "Sounded fine to me. Better than what I could've done, anyway."

"It was lame, I could've easily done better," piped up Luna, a grin on her face.

"Always glad to know I can improve," said Junell, chuckling as he walked past the two, off the stage.

—

Commander Wisle crumpled down to the white marble floor of the castle, blood pouring from his back. Out of his stomach protruded a katana; a golden katana, the one wielded by Commander Dreid. As the katana came back out, even more blood started to gush out of the wound, staining the once beautiful floor red. Wisle fell to the ground, rolling onto his back, trying to see his killer in his final moments. It was Dreid; standing over him, a devilish grin plastered on his smug face.

"*Dread...* w-why...?" choked out Wisle, confused.

Dreid turned around, not caring to look at the bloody, writhing mass that spoke to him.

"With you gone, I will be the commander of Bastea. I will be the ruler of Terre! The fate of this kingdom now belongs to me!"

Dreid cackled with glee. He'd been an underling to Ranken for too long. He was stronger than Ranken, the fat geezer, so it only made sense. The only thing that stopped him was the thousands of loyal guards he had. But now that Ranken was missing, and his top commander assassinated, there was no one left on the totem pole of power. It was Dreid's turn to rule.

He turned around, looking at the body of

Wisle. The weakling was only his superior as he knew Ranken from long ago. Dreid had been a rising star, but was new, and relatively unknown in the Devil cult. He moved forward then gave the body a solid kick. It felt good; the years of being under Wisle's command infuriated him. Wisle was a terrible commander; he barely knew how to coordinate fights, usually letting the sergeants figure it out. It was probably his fault the rebels grew so strong, what with his lack of strategy.

But now, Dreid would rule. He would command the army as he saw fit; he'd kill every single rebel, stomp out any resistance. Rule with an iron fist. The grin returned to his face. Yes, make the populace fear him. Fear the Devil's cult once again.

"Uh—"

The guard froze, startled by the ghastly sight in front of him. Commander Dreid stood above Commander Wisle, who lay dead, some of his organs visibly coming out from the large hole in his stomach.

Dreid turned his attention to the guard, whose mouth was agape, clearly in shock.

"What, soldier? Spit it out!"

The guard, regaining his composure, and struggling not to look at the dead commander's body, responded. "A messenger has arrived, sir. Castle Yvyerst has fallen!"

Dreid grimaced, gnashing his teeth. It was a double ruse—not only was the siege fake, but they had also directed their army towards Western Terre! It slowly dawned on him that the four cardinal regions were now controlled by the rebels. They'd surely be preparing an attack on Bastea now.

"Shore up the defenses. They will siege Bastea soon. Go!"

The guard nodded, making sure to not look Dreid in the eye, then ran off, his boots clanging loudly on the marble hall of the castle.

Well, now was the time to prove his skill.

He was the best commander of all of Terre; he'd never lost a battle. This would be no different. *No person on Terre can defeat me—no one!*

CHAPTER 18

Kingdom's end

Lucifer and Luna were headed to Bastea, alone, not part of any contingents. Their mission was to be done in secret; it was the same one they'd always done—assassination. The new ruler of Terre, King Dreid, was previously Ranken's best commander. He had led the Devil's cult to countless victories in Western and Southern Terre; he was the likely reason they were able to defeat King Bastea all those years ago. Knowing this made this the hardest challenge yet. Dreid would play smart; he'd be giving commands from afar, hidden from the battlefield. If they were to find him, eliminate him, they'd be able to remove strategy from the castle defense, giving the ground troops a much easier job in breaking into the castle.

Lucifer could feel Luna's hands gripped onto his waist. Her hands felt delicate even though they wore an armoured gauntlet. He loved spending every moment with her. Soon, however, they would be on the battlefield. He wanted to watch over her, make sure she was safe. But she constantly told him to trust her; that she could handle herself. For the sake of the troops outside the walls, they had to split up to cover ground faster. For the faster they eliminated Dreid, the more lives they would be able to save.

Yet the only thing on his mind was the feeling of her body resting on his back. It was warm; comforting. *If only this could go on forever.*

–

Dreid saw the first signs of danger to the south. Legions of men on their warhorses, racing towards Castle Bastea. They rode quickly, halberds raised up, war cries thundering across the vast plain between them and the castle walls.

He wrote down a note on a piece of paper, then attached it to a pigeon. The pigeon flew off, knowing where it must go. Dreid stood in the highest tower of Bastea, what once was a single-celled prison. It was a great vantage point to measure the battle, with windows to all directions; and, being up so high, far away from the reach of any arrow. It was the perfect spot to defend Castle Bastea from.

–

The castle walls loomed ahead; signs of war were clearly visible, flames pouring over the rampart walls, arrows from the ground flying to meet the unlucky soldiers who didn't keep their heads down enough.

Lucifer and Luna were on one of King Rakcizs' siege towers. The giant siege towers, made of wood and steel, would protect them from arrows until they were close enough to get onto the eastern wall.

Whizz.

Whizz...

Thunk!

A crossbow bolt slammed into the wooden armour of the siege tower. It vibrated the tower slightly, but was otherwise unharmed by the large dart. Lucifer was knelt down, behind the armour, looking at the sky. He was focusing on the still clouds; once he could no longer see them, he'd know the tower would be in range.

Whizz...

Thunk.

Thunk!

A large arrow smacked into the opposite side of the armour that Lucifer had his head behind. The resounding sound was loud. They were close. He peered up at the clouds again; it was gone! It was time to enter the castle.

Lucifer motioned to Luna with his hand, then got up. They were only meters away from the castle wall. He could see Dreid's men milling about, reloading crossbows, firing arrows, desperately trying to fend off the wave of siege towers that were approaching. Not wasting any time, Luna jumped on Lucifer's back, ready to go. Lucifer *flew* over the gap to the top of the wall ramparts, landing in the midst of enemy soldiers.

Did I... did I see an almost invisible wing?

Luna had no time to think about what she saw; she rolled off and laid low. Lucifer swung his longsword around, cleaving in two the enemies closest to them. Then, Lucifer rushed the wall to the south, clearing it of panicking archers. Luna went north, doing the same.

–

Noticing that the siege towers had breached the eastern wall, Dreid quickly scribbled down something on another piece of paper then attached it to a waiting pigeon. The pigeon flew off frantically. He frowned. The siege towers hadn't been stopped by the ballistae or archers like he'd hoped. Now he would have to rely on the inside forces to defend the ramparts. The battle was already swaying away from his favour, and he did not like that.

A different pigeon, laden with a note on its leg, flew to the tower window. *The battle was going by too quickly,* thought Dreid, *what's the matter now?* Dreid removed the note, then unfolded it; it read:

> *king*
>
> *terror inside*
>
> *— s.g.*

It took but a moment for the message to dawn on Dreid. The Terror Knight was inside the castle already—most likely looking for him. Dreid yelled out into the void; in anger, frustration, fear. This couldn't be the end of him. He had only just become king—it wasn't fair. *Oh, lord Satan, give me your strength in this trying time.*

–

The wooden wall in front of Luna was all too famil-iar; the courtyard wall. She jumped forward, grabbed hold of the top with her hands, then clambered over. Lucifer was wreaking havoc on the streets; most of the guards were either after him or running away from him. The ones in Luna's way, however, she dispatched of efficiently enough.

She was heading for the tallest tower in Bastea; the prison cell, the very one she had once been imprisoned in. She recalled the stellar view it had of the entire castle grounds. It would be a great place to command an army, and so she suspected the new king or a commander might be there.

The rusty wheelbarrow she had climbed up the first time was still there; the trimmed bushes, sturdy as ever. She carefully crawled on the top until she reached the garden roof; there, ahead, was the wall she had once climbed—and fallen from.

This time it wasn't raining, however. It was dry and sunny. She grabbed a window ledge, pulled herself up, put her feet on the ledge, then proceeded to climb to the next window. Bit by bit she went higher.

Don't look down.

Focus.

Luna reached the final window—on the sixth floor. Now, to continue her journey up the tower, she'd have to enter inside and find the way up. She smashed the window with the hilt of her longsword, the shattering glass dancing on the marble floor. She climbed in, quickly making notice of her surroundings. It was a library, filled with books, but devoid of any humans. She looked to the left—there was the door—and ran over. The door was locked; she stood back, gathering her strength, then lunged forward, smashing into the door with her right shoulder pauldron. The wooden door flung wide open, exposing a white-marbled hallway. She quickly glanced around, looking for the stairs. *Yes, over there.* She spotted a small entranceway with a staircase behind it. She ran over, eager to see what lay ahead.

–

Dreid had his binoculars up; he was staring at some- thing very intently. What he saw, on the castle streets, was a knight, fast as the wind, cutting down his soldiers in a blur. *The Terror.* It could not pos- sibly be human. It had to be a monster; that would explain its feats. He put the binoculars down, sigh- ing. He knew the battle would soon be lost. He would need to find a way to escape, just like Ranken had.

The basement…
Yes, the basement.

Ranken's guard. The only one to ever be seen again. If what he spoke of was actually true, and not just the drunken ramblings of a madman, Dreid might still have a chance to survive. There was no other way, not when the entire castle was surrounded. He'd have to take his chances.

Step...

Step...

Step...

Dreid jolted his head, hearing the footsteps. They were coming from the spiral staircase that led to the tower. No one was supposed to know he was in here—so who, or what, could it be? He unsheathed his katana, preparing for what was to come.

—

As Luna reached the tower door, her ears picked up a rustle from inside. There was someone inside—that she now knew. She closed her eyes briefly, thinking of a plan. When none came to mind, she shook her head. *Doesn't matter; don't overthink it. Just do.*

She kicked open the door; what met her was the thin blade of a katana, which she only just dodged. The wielder of the blade, Dreid, retracted his blade and prepared for another strike. Luna, seeing this, ducked down and ran low. Dreid's katana blade glanced off her right pauldron, leaving a damaged groove on the dark armour. Luna turned around, swinging her longsword horizontally. Dreid met her blade with his own, parrying the blow.

"So, they sent an assassin against me, have they?" cried out Dreid, raising his katana for another swing. Luna barely managed to block the attack when Dreid threw out another cut. His attacks were lightning-fast; she didn't know if she could keep defending successfully.

Then, as she blocked another attack once again, Dreid lunged forward, pressing Luna backwards. As she stumbled back, her back suddenly felt empty air; there was no support there. It was a window.

Dreid, seizing the advantage, crossed their weapons upward. Seeing a weak spot, he kneed

Luna in her unprotected belly.

Luna groaned in pain, almost letting go of her longsword; the blow was painful, coming from Dreid's metal kneepad. She never wore anything over her stomach, preferring the agility and flexibility it gave. But right now, its weakness showed.

Dreid pulled his knee back, ready to smack the weak spot again. As he thrust forward, he suddenly felt himself lose purchase with the floor. He looked up; Luna had let go of her longsword and slid to the right, causing Dreid to fall into the window from his own force. As he desperately attempted to turn around, he felt a shove on his back, finally ejecting him out the window. His screams fell onto deaf ears; soon replaced with a loud *thump,* the sound of his body smashing into the garden roof, far, far below.

—

Lucifer had cleared the streets. There were commanders there, but no King Dreid. He wasn't directing his troops from below, so he had to be some-where up high. The highest point in Bastea was a spiral tower near the center. Lucifer headed towards there, fast; fast enough that a wave of turbulence followed his wake, sweeping up leaves into large temporary clouds. It was the only earthly reminder of his presence to the citizens who were huddled in their homes, who only saw a blur fly by their win-dows.

He soon reached the base of the tower. There was the courtyard; a long, wooden wall pro-tected it, however, measuring two and a half meters tall. Lucifer jumped over it with ease, landing on the grassy other side. It was when he lifted his head he saw the sword.

It was a silver longsword. It was *Luna's.*

Lucifer froze, staring at the sword, which lay on the garden floor. He shook his head, clearing his head, then ran towards it. It lay on the ground stained with blood. *But whose blood?*

Luna was nowhere in sight. Did the sword fall from above? He looked up, towards the tower. In the process of doing so, he noticed a large hole in the garden roof. He picked up Luna's sword, then ran over to investigate, heart beating in his chest with fear.

The hole was human-shaped. Looking down, he could now see the body. The dead man wore golden armour, the same ones a king would wear. His insignia was that of the Bastean Ruler.

This must be King Dreid... and he's dead.

Lucifer looked up; past the hole in the roof, and to the tower. Dreid must have fallen from the top of the spiral tower. Someone pushed him off; but if Luna's sword was also on the ground, then...

"Lucifer!"

The familiar, soft yet raspy voice broke his trance. Lucifer turned around, and there was Luna— perfectly fine. He ran to her, dropping the two swords he held, then gave her a big embrace. Luna returned it back, burying her head into his chest, perhaps to hide the water coming from her eyes.

"I told you to trust me," she said, stifling her tears. He did trust her, but fighting alone was scary and dangerous—too dangerous.

He held her in his embrace for a while before responding.

"I trust you. But it never hurts to ask for help."

–

As the cheers of the crowd waned in the distance, Junell approached Lucifer. He was standing on the castle wall, with Luna, as usual. Junell knelt down, then cleared his throat, before speaking.

"Lucifer... my lord, you have every right to become King of Terre," said Junell. He lowered his gaze down, bowing his head to the knight.

"You've led us to victory over the Devil's cult. You've earned it. No, you deserve it."

Lucifer slowly turned his head to look at

Junell. He shook his head. "Stand up. Junell. You should be king. I wouldn't know where to start as king of Terre. You have experience leading as well —the people already look up to you."

Junell carefully stood up, aghast at Lucifer's decision. "You… you don't want to be king? I'd think anyone would…"

Lucifer, in his patented emotionless tone, responded.

"I don't want to, believe me—King Junell."

CHAPTER 19

Meeting Death

It had been a week since the victory at Bastea. Lucifer was given a room in Castle Bastea; here he stood, on the balcony, looking at the moonlight. It was a quiet night; Luna was bathing herself, so he had decided to enjoy the fresh air for a bit.

A shadowy figure caught his attention. It came from the ground, far away; it floated upwards, towards him. Lucifer, startled, turned around and ran to get his sword. He drew it out of its sheath then ran back onto the balcony. The shadowy apparition came closer; it seemed familiar. Lucifer had seen it before; but where?

The message at Gruppen!

The being who had warned him of Luna's perilous capture. The hooded figure who wielded a reaper; *the Grim Reaper*.

The shadowy figure had finally reached the balcony. Now level with Lucifer, it spoke.

"My lord…"

It seemed to pause; for effect, perhaps, before it continued.

"...you are ready to come home."

–

His name was Grim; he was the Grim Reaper, the bringer of death. He served what Terrans called God: Satan. Grim had kept a close eye on Lucifer ever since he was banished to the overworld, watching his progress, but not interfering. He wanted to see if the child survived. Lucifer had far surpassed his expectations. Even when faced with adversity, the child had trudged on, fighting for the right cause. His actions showed that he was a great person —far greater than his father.

There were, of course, many questions that Lucifer had for Grim. He answered a few. But not all answers could be so easily explained. For them, Lucifer would need to see them with his own eyes. He'd need to go to the underworld.

"Tell me, how would I go there?" asked Lucifer, incredulous. The past few minutes he had spent with Grim only made him more confused. His father, Satan, creator of the world. He wouldn't have believed it, were it not for his own supernatural abilities.

"Deep, very deep in this castle, is a path into the underworld. Created a millennia ago… all but forgotten," spoke Grim.

"And you'll show me where it is?"

"Worry not, my lord."

–

Luna looked at Grim, then back to Lucifer. All of this was scary and it didn't make much sense. But at the same time, it did. His growing strength, his insane power. Lucifer was no human; he was something else. She nodded to Lucifer, giving him her approval.

"We're ready, Grim," replied Lucifer.

"Well then, my lord. Prepare to see your true father—Satan."

—

Deep in a secret passageway in the basement of Castle Bastea lay a magical portal. The path to it was long, dark, and frightening. The closer one would get, the stronger the thick mist became, and the more nerve-wracking the experience was. Get close enough, and one would hear a trickle of water coming from above, an unnerving constant.

The portal itself was pitch black. Surrounding it was a polished metal frame, ever so softly glowing, indicating it was unnatural. The water, from the darkness above, pooled at the bottom and flowed into the portal's hole.

Grim led the way, a magical purple flame

lighting up the path ahead of them. Lucifer held dearly onto Luna, terrified of the darkness. Luna, used to being in darkness from her upbringing in the forest of evil, comforted him, once in a while patting him on his shoulder.

The mist became thick; it smelled of... fire. Flames. Something like burning coal, but sootier, more toxic.

Then, the purple light held by Grim reflected off a shiny frame in the distance: the portal. They moved until they were in front of it; inside the portal was completely dark—nothing reflected off of it. Grim turned his ghostly body around, facing Lucifer.

"The portal, my lord."

Grim floated forward, passing half of his body through the portal. The other half, which remained in Terre, beckoned to Lucifer.

"Come, my lord. Your destiny awaits you."

Lucifer took a step forward, then hesitated.

This was too crazy. But then again, his abilities were crazy; his strength, speed.

He had to know the truth.

He then looked towards Luna, who stared back at him with her sparkly green eyes. This wasn't her journey to take; he didn't know how dangerous it was going to be from here on out.

"You don't have to go with me, darling—"

Luna interrupted him, almost as if she expected him to say something like this.

"Am I not safer in your presence?"

On her face was a wry smile. He was always saying this; if he left her behind, he'd be contradicting himself.

Lucifer stepped towards her, holding her hand.

"Of course."

They both slowly walked into the portal together. As they went through, the sound of dripping water slowly dwindled, until it disappeared altogether.

–

The underworld was quite dark, but the sky was illuminated by a fiery red glow. All around the raised rock platform they stood on was an unending valley of lava, filled with small dots, seeming to bob up and down the lava. Ahead of them was a rock bridge; the only path forward. As they walked down it, Grim nonchalantly explained what was going on.

"Those who died, who lived a bad life, are sent into the lava ocean. They are born into the lava you see all around you. They will feel pain and die in the lava. Then, once they die, the cycle repeats, never to end."

Lucifer's eyes widened, horrified at the thought. The little dots in the lava—they were all people. He couldn't hear them, but they were probably screaming in pain. *For eternity.*

Grim continued his monologue.

"This was devised by Satan as a way to

punish the undeserving. A very, very long time ago, now. I can't imagine the pain the first one to spawn there must be feeling. Yes, the first one is down there, somewhere, dying over and over again."

Grim, seeing Lucifer's body language shift slightly at the mention of Satan, changed the direction of the one-way conversation.

"Ah, the heavenly father, the holy spirit; God. That is He, the holy being. His name is Satan; king of the underworld, creator of all, ender of all. Your father."

Grim paused for a moment, thinking of what to say next. Satisfied with his thoughts, he continued.

"Let me tell you a story. The story of God."

–

"Long, long ago, God created this world. In it, he created humans: they were of his image. He left them to their own devices, to see what they would do; to entertain himself. They fought, killed, loved, built, you know... what humans do. He was enamoured by what he saw. I was brought along to bring the souls of the dead to the underworld. There, the pure humans became humble servants of him; the bad would spawn in the lava and suffer for eternity. Those who he considered neutral? Their souls would disappear, never to be seen again. A better fate than to be reborn a slave, some might say.

Thousands of years went by, and Satan got bored of his little experiment. He had long left his loyal servant, Grim—me, in other words—, to take care of the humans, overworld and underworld alike. The humans weren't so interesting to watch anymore; he'd seen everything there was to see. He wanted something for himself. He wanted to experience what humans called love; something he *didn't* create, but *somehow* created.

So, he created what he thought was the perfect mate and brought her to life. Her name was Lumia. And for a thousand years, she was the perfect wife.

Something that was always in the back of his mind were the strange words told to him when he created the world of Terre. It was a prophetic poem that appeared in his head.

> *The child of the devil,*
> *Languishes at his peril.*
> *He who shall seek retribution,*
> *On the father of creation.*

From where or whence this prophecy came from, even Satan did not know. What wasn't up for debate was what the poem foretold—the child of Satan would come for his head.

Satan knew he couldn't have a child. He was immortal; he didn't need one. He didn't create himself to be able to do so. So, he was never worried.

However, on the first day of the thousandth year of their marriage, Lumia became pregnant. Satan grew worried; his child would replace him;

kill him, take his place as god. He was afraid of this child. His love for Lumia, however, stopped him from killing her right then and there.

When the child was born, it was a girl. Satan sighed with relief then. A girl could never replace him; never kill him. A girl could not become a god. Only one in the same image as Satan could; he was safe, for now, at least.

But Lumia might have another child. It might be a boy next time, and who knows when she would get pregnant. Maybe it was a thousand years from then, maybe the next day.

As the days passed, Satan grew more fearful until one day, he killed her. He killed Lumia.

Now, without a wife, Satan grew restless. He wanted to sleep with women again; but only perfect ones, ones like Lumia. So, he tried to remember Lumia's face, and created two more; Melanie and Risa.

Beautiful as they were, neither matched

Lumia. For years Satan was dejected, sleeping with his new wives, but never feeling the same as he did for Lumia.

On his daughter's eighteenth birthday, he finally met his child. He had refused to see her growing up; as such, his reaper, Grim (yes, that's me again), raised her.

When Satan saw her, he was startled. She looked remarkably so like Lumia; she was her spitting image. Satan would become happy once again.

For another thousand years, all was well. Satan ignored his other wives, instead focusing his attention on Lucia. If you wonder, yes, I thought it *weird* for Satan to marry his own daughter; but as my lord, I could not object.

And on that thousandth and first day… You, Lucifer, were born.

'Twas only a month until Satan found out. In a rage, he killed your mother, poor Lucia. As a second God, he couldn't kill you in the underworld.

So, he sent you to the overworld to die, where you would lose your powers, not having matured yet.

Unfortunately for him, while his choice of location was actually quite good, a certain general and his men were returning from war at that same moment, unwittingly saving you.

This is your story, my lord. It is up to you to decide what pages will be written next."

CHAPTER 20

Duel of two Gods

Ranken screamed in pain. He had been constantly spawning a few meters above the lava, only to fall into it, then get burned to death or drown inside the lava. His final cries went unnoticed, as it was joined by thousands of other screams from the other people meeting the same fate.

Then, the cycle started all over again.

Ranken had but a second to scream before he fell into the lava again, drowning. He burst up to the surface, lungs burnt, unable to scream.

Then, the cycle started all over again.

He looked up, perhaps for the thousandth time, into the red sky. His mind had only a second to think of regrets before he plunged back into the lava.

Then, the cycle started all over again.

He looked up, perhaps for the thousandth and first time, towards the rock bridge. The very bridge which led him to this fate. He should've never entered the portal. He plunged into the lava, his screeches drowned out by everyone else's.

Then, the cycle started all over again.

He looked at the bridge and saw something familiar. A tall knight, dressed in all black armour— and the girl, the succubus he caught in that castle courtyard! Then he plunged into the lava.

Then, the cycle started all over again.

He screamed towards them, trying to get their attention. Now, he needed them to help him. But his voice got lost in the sea of screams around him, and he once again plunged into the lava.

Then, the cycle started all over again.

—

Lucifer kept walking, going ever closer to the castle. What Grim had said was stuck in his mind. It was all too crazy to even think of right now. He should focus on the task ahead. *Do I... kill Satan? My destiny is to seek retribution. What does that entail?* It seemed like a self-fulfilling destiny to Lucifer. Satan had killed his mother *and* grandmother. Who wouldn't want to exact revenge? Just like how he wanted to kill Ranken for causing the death of his mother.

He had already asked Grim about his adoptive parents. When they came, where did they go? To the good side, the bad, or neither? Grim, having the responsibility of so many people, didn't remember. Lucifer knew his parents were good, though. They had to have gone to the good side; they had to be in the underworld, somewhere.

"Tell me, Grim, why did you do nothing to stop Satan?" piped up Luna. She was curious as to why Grim always seemed to be on the sidelines of the story.

"I am loyal to God only. Everything I do, I must consider him first," he responded, politely.

Luna, confused, asked another question. "Then why are you helping Lucifer, if he plans to go against Satan? Perhaps even kill him?"

Grim replied without skipping a beat. "Lord Lucifer is 'God' too. I must be loyal to both."

"That... doesn't make too much sense," remarked Luna. If both were fighting to the death, who would Grim help? Neither of them? She looked at Lucifer, who was staring ahead at the castle. She'd step in, then, if Satan overpowered him. She probably wouldn't stand a chance against a god, but she'd do anything for Lucifer.

—

During their journey to Satan's castle, they passed by a few towns, filled with people. They bowed down their heads to Grim as the group walked by. Lucifer had looked for his parents, but failed to find them. Soon enough though, they had arrived at

Satan's residence: a very long, tall building, made of a dark stone, with windows spanning its front face.

The castle guards stood up straighter and clanked their weapons on the ground when the group passed by them. They didn't know who the two followers were, but they knew Grim—the second in command.

Grim, with a flick of his ghostly hand, magically opened the gates and doors of Satan's castle without effort. As the three walked through the massive halls of the castle, servants and workers stopped their duties to bow down. The two humans behind the ghastly figure mattered not. The presence of the reaper, Grim, however, commanded respect.

Upon seeing the giant doorway of the throne room, Lucifer stopped. He could turn back now; leave this place, live a peaceful life in the overworld. Forget about Satan; pretend he didn't exist. Then, he thought of his birth mother, Lucia. The other wives of Satan, would they be his stepmothers? They could be in danger too, although they'd never gotten pregnant over the millennia. Lucifer prepared himself, then continued walking forward. He had made up his mind.

–

"Hm, this wine tastes quite poor. ANOTHER ONE," hammered out Satan. The maid briskly carried the wine bottle and scurried out the now-open throne room door. Open... door.

The door was closed a moment ago. Satan inched his head forward to see who opened it. No one was supposed to be coming in; or maybe it was Grim, who came at random times, randomly.

Grim floated in, bowing down. Ah, yes. It was Grim—

Trailing behind Grim were two people he'd never seen before. Satan looked around, scowling, before demanding an answer from his servant.

"GRIM! Who are these... strangers?"

Grim, still bowing, replied.

"The lady is Lady Luna, a succubus."

Satan stared at her. She was beautiful—very much so. But her mouth… it wasn't human. No, not something Satan liked.

"The knight is named Lucifer."

The armoured knight stood tall, staring right back at Satan. That was definitely a sign of disrespect, a sign of *dominance*. Satan frowned. Did this fool not know who he was standing in front of?

"Hello… father," spoke Lucifer.

Satan froze. Through the eye slots of the knight's helmet, he could see the man's eyes. Lucifer's eyes glowed red with fury, producing light like only a god could do.

It couldn't be… my son?

—

Satan stood up abruptly, startling his two wives behind him. One held her hand to her mouth, the other accidentally dropped the fanning leaf she was holding.

"What is the meaning of this, Grim? You mean to tell me my son is alive all this time?" said Satan, incredulous.

Grim, still bowing, replied.

"Yes, sire."

"And you never finished him off?" thundered Satan, incredulous.

"No, sire."

"WHY NOT???" shouted Satan, furious.

"He is God too, sire. My commands are to serve God, always."

Satan shook his head. It was kind of his fault, to be honest, but he didn't want to admit it. Grim should have some self-thinking up there, somewhere in his empty ghost head. Now the prophecy was going to become true.

With a brilliant flash of light, Satan summoned his giant cleaver sword. Then, a large, dark, right wing suddenly shot out of his back, opening instantly. Shocked, his wives scuttled backwards, huddling together in fear. Lucifer waved for Luna to get back as well. A duel of two gods was about to commence.

Grim stood up, nodded to both gods, then floated away. Whatever happened next would decide the fate of both worlds. It wasn't up to him to decide who won, only to serve whoever survived the encounter.

—

Satan's single wing flapped once; he flew forward with the speed of lightning. Now at his full power, Lucifer saw the attack and instantly blocked it. Satan swung again and again; powerful, thundering clashes filled the room. Luna ran towards the two huddled ladies and escorted them out of the throne room, which was now a battleground.

"You will not replace me!" shrieked Satan, pummeling away at Lucifer. *HE* created this world. Not his kid. It was *HIS* world to rule. He would not lose to this so-called 'Lucifer'.

Lucifer parried Satan's attack then started to counterattack with his own slashes. Both matched each other's pace, blades loudly clanging as metal ground against metal; sparks flying, massive amounts of heat being generated.

"I've trained all my life for this, Satan. You will go down," said Lucifer, clenching his teeth.

Satan, blocking blows, could only laugh at the absurd statement.
"Oh really? You think so? I created this WORLD, *son*, your training means nothing—"

Lucifer had cut horizontally at Satan's legs, causing him to block. Upon doing so, Lucifer raised his leg and kicked Satan's stomach, sending him flying backwards and smashing into a pillar. Satan hadn't predicted that move; he thought Lucifer would only be using his sword.

Satan groaned. Was this… pain he felt? Impossible! He was God. But there was no time to recover. Lucifer had now activated his own wing; it was a large, silver left wing.

With a single flap, Lucifer dashed forward, his deadly blade pointed directly at Satan. He was going for a charging stab, moving so fast he was but a blur.

Satan rolled on the floor, causing Lucifer's stab to miss and pierce the pillar, smashing it into pieces. Satan quickly stood back up, slashing at where Lucifer was. But he wasn't there anymore. The pillar was gone; Lucifer had gone completely through it.

Lucifer flew around across the room's perimeter with a dizzying speed, disorientating Satan, who struggled to keep track of where he went. Then, he threw his giant sword at Satan.

Satan blocked the dark-silver sword and watched it clang to the ground. Surely Lucifer wasn't that dumb? There was no way that would work.

"You know, you almost got me. Then you had to do some dumb shit like throw your fucking sword away. You know you lost now, don't cha?" cackled Satan.

Lucifer smiled at Satan, then spoke.

"Laughing while you still can, I see."

Satan was taken aback, and frowned. Was his son delusional? Was he crazy? Was he out of his mind? He clearly had no weapon anymore.

"You know, I really don't know what you're thinking, You LITERALLY threw away your WEAPON, did you HEAR—"

STAB.

Blood. Pain.

Satan looked down at the source. There was a throbbing pain in his chest. There was… a silver sword in his chest. It had entered from behind. Satan slowly turned around to see what happened. There stood Luna, a cruel grin on her face. She then stepped back, away from Satan.

"That little ploy was to distract you. I figured you'd be laughing so hard you wouldn't notice me coming up from behind you," she smirked.

Satan fell to his knees, unable to summon any words.

Lucifer walked up towards him, picked his sword back off the ground, then pointed it at Satan.

With blood now coming out of his mouth, Satan garbled out something, barely intelligible. "Shit… fusgds..! Hguh, fucking… you fuck… shgfh…"

It appeared as though he was in pain; perhaps in pain for the first time. Despite being a 'lethal' strike, the sword in his abdomen was unable to kill him, being wielded by Luna, who was not a god. The only being that could kill Satan was Lucifer.

Lucifer raised his sword up—and in one fell swoop, sheathed his sword.

"No. I control my own fate, not you, not some prophecy. Not anyone else," said Lucifer. His father's words still rang true in his mind. His *real* father, not Satan.

Then he took Luna's sword out of Satan, the wrong way out though, so the hilt also went through his body.

"ARGH! WHAT THE FUCK???" screamed Satan.

Lucifer handed back the sword to Luna before responding. "Be glad it was only pain rather than death... *'father'*.

CHAPTER 21

A missing soul

The couple now had a home within the vast castle of the underworld. With it, they had loyal servants ready to tend to their needs at a moment's notice, now that Lucifer was anointed as God. Lucifer, however, had only need of one—Grim.

He had yet to find his parents, Lenkl and Mary. And so, he sought out the underworld's gate-keeper, to see if the ghostly figure had any more information. The last time he'd asked, Grim was going off of memory, and didn't recall.

The office was small, dim, full of ancient books. Miniature candles laced the walls, filling the room with their burning scent. There sat Grim, in the center of the room, writing away at a logbook. Hearing that someone had entered, he peeked up; noticing it was Lucifer, with Luna trailing behind him, he quickly stood—no, floated—up, and took a deep bow.

"My Lord. For what reason do you grace me with your presence?" he asked, closing his logbook.

Lucifer walked towards a bit before speaking. "I wish to find my parents. I cannot seem to find them. Don't you have logs of some kind, that has the names of everyone in the underworld?"

Grim nodded. "Aye, that I do. Three books for the three types of souls. Let me fetch them, and I'll see what I can find."

Grim turned around, walked to his large bookshelf, and began rummaging through it.

"You won't need the book of the, what do you call it," said Lucifer, trying to think of what those in the ocean of lava were called.

"The book of the damned? Alright. Ah, here

is the book of souls. And... here is the book of the dead."

Grim held two books in his hands. One was tinted blue; the other, tinted black.

"Give me some time, and I'll tell you when I've found their names."

—

Lucifer sat in the hallway outside Grim's office, tense. He knew his parents were good people. They had to be. His mother was always kind to everyone; his father always taught him lessons of life, how to be a better person. Luna sat beside him, patting his leg, comforting him. "There, there. I'm sure your parents made it out on the good side."

Lucifer nodded, but said nothing. He'd searched a few towns already in the underworld. There were no hints of his parents in any of them. But enough lamenting about himself; what about Luna? She had never talked about her parents, her upbringing. Lucifer looked at her and asked.

"Luna, what about your parents? Do you wonder what happened to them?

Luna shook her head, a wistful look in her eyes. "I have no memories of them. Nor do I know their names. I don't think Grim could find them if he tried."

Now it was Lucifer's turn to comfort Luna. He wrapped his arms around her shoulder. She leaned her head into his arm, closing her eyes. The only person she needed was her Lucifer.

A shuffle from inside the office broke captured the couple's attention. Soon, out walked Grim, no books in hand this time. The ghostly man coughed a bit, covering his mouth with a fist, before speaking.

"My Lord, Mary Deniere resides in a nearby town. But..." he paused before bringing the bad news. "Lenkl Deniere is written down in the book of dead. He is gone."

Lucifer's face stood rigid, emotionless. His

father, gone? How? He was an honourable man—it couldn't be true. Lucifer's mind went back to when he was a child, when his father taught him fighting lessons.

"A noble knight does not needlessly kill, Lucifer."

"Why? What if they tried to kill me?"

"It matters not, my son. If they've sur-rendered, they pose no more threat to you."

Lenkl's life wasn't easy. In the wars Lenkl had fought, he had faced hard times. Many difficult choices had to be made—many which could've affected the lives of the men under his control. He made those decisions, whether good or bad, to save his men. He was only human, after all. In this world that Satan had created, even if you fought for the side of justice, you could still do wrong.

Lucifer closed his eyes, breathing out.

"Take me to my mother."

—

The lady had sat on the bench for how many days now? She 'd been waiting for her husband to show up, but he never did. The townsfolk often tried to tell her he was probably long gone, but she'd never listen. She would give them a smile, say nothing, and return to the bench. Today would be no different.

A few passersby waved to her. Seeing them, she waved back. Every day that they walked by, she was there, sitting on the bench, alone. They felt for her. Everyone here had someone they'd thought would come through, but didn't. They knew the pain she was in, the pain she was hiding away.

Lenkl, my dearest, any day now.

Mary hummed a small tune she had often sung around Castle Gruppen. It brought her comfort, reminiscing about days long gone. When she first met the young lord, marrying him. When she found out she couldn't have a child, and the sorrow thereafter. When he went off to war, and her fear knew no bounds. When Lenkl found their son in the forest, the joy she had elicited. All these and more, waiting to be shared with, to be remembered with. With her husband, Lenkl.

"Miss Deniere."

Mary looked up, surprised. She had never told anyone here her last name. That would mean whoever spoke knew her from when she was living. But this man in front of her... oh, it was Grim. Grim knew everyone, of course. He was the one who brought their souls to the underworld. She bowed her head in respect to the ghostly figure. "Master Grim. To what do I owe you for your appearance?"

"Lucifer."

Behind Grim stood a towering knight with horrific armour. Beside him, a succubus, her wide mouth smiling creepily at her. *As if she wants to eat me!* thought Mary. She looked at the two, unsure. The knight's name must be Lucifer, then. The same name her son has. She looked back at the succubus, thinking that she looked familiar. *I think I've seen her before. But where?*

The knight took off his ghoulish helmet, revealing his face. There, in front of her, stood her son. Lucifer. Mary jumped up and hugged him in sheer joy. She had tears in her eyes; she'd thought she'd never see him again. But why was he here...?

"My dear, why... why are you here?"

"To see you, mother," said Lucifer, confused. Was she not happy to see him? Was she mad he failed to save her in time?

Luna interjected, "She probably means why are you in the underworld. Fears you died, most likely."

–

Mary nodded her head, as if understanding, but in reality, not really. Her dear son was the son of God. He had told her of his journey to save her; how he ended up saving Bastea, and now returned to his rightful home in the underworld. He also introduced her to his girlfriend, the succubus. Mary was scared of the lady at first, but after hearing the times she'd saved her son, became grateful for the lady with the monstrous mouth.

–

They waited at the edge of town. Grim was to return any moment now, with a gift for Mary. What it was, none of them had any idea. Grim had said it suddenly, as if he remembered something. Then he told them to wait here. Five minutes later, he returned.

In tow was a raggedy man who looked like a crow. The man was being dragged along by Grim, who seemed to have a smile on his ghostly face.

"Ah, Mary. Here is someone you may recognize," said Grim.

"How dare you! Let me go!" complained the raggedy man.

Mary stared at him, unsure what to make of him. He looked kind of familiar, but she wasn't too sure who it was. Hm, maybe if the clothes weren't so raggedly, he would look like a... count. Count Creiz!?

"Go ahead, give him a good kick to the groin," said Grim. Mary looked around, unsure of herself. She had never kicked anyone before. "Come on now, he's due to return to the lava any minute now," hurried Grim.

"You don't dare touch me! Y-you, Anne, was it? Uh, Madeline?" said a confused Count Creiz.

Mary walked over to Creiz and gave him a good, hard kick to the balls. Creiz cried out in pain.

"Let go of me! Let go of me NOW! I'll beat your ass! You coward!" shrieked an unhappy Creiz

Mary winded up another kick, then SLAM. The Count doubled over in pain, screaming, before suddenly fading away.

"Oh, that's all the time he had. He's back to the lava ocean now," said Grim. "Hope you enjoyed that."

Mary nodded. She enjoyed that a lot. Her last days on Terre were miserable due to that man. It felt good to have her revenge, even if it were to take place in the underworld.

CHAPTER 22

To become immortal

Lucifer kissed Luna, then lifted her up and spun her around. They were now married. Grim was speaking in the back, reading off words from the pages of the marriage book, but no one was listening to him drone on and on. Mary, Melanie, and Risa stood to the side, shedding tears of joy for the newlyweds. Satan wasn't there, content with never seeing Lucifer again.

Satan was spared by Lucifer, who was unwilling to kill his helpless opponent. Satan was furious at the loss, but being unable to overpower Lucifer, he could do nothing about it.

Lucifer would watch over the overworld;

intervene when things got ugly, bad, when things went out of control. Satan would stick to the under-world, doing whatever he pleased; watching dead people suffer in lava, bringing them up to torture them, basically anything sadistic. The two could not be more different.

"You know, darling, you're a god. You could always fix my mouth if you wanted to," said Luna to Lucifer. The look in his eyes indicated that he was thinking of something.

He looked at her, her terrifying mouth in a big grin, her shark-like teeth shining brightly. No, there was nothing he'd change about her. She was a succubus, a monster, a She-Devil, the Demon Maiden. She was Luna; his everything—and she was perfect the way she was.

–

As he lay in his bed, Lucifer had troubling thoughts. He should be happy; everything he had set out to do, he had completed. He learned of his true identity: he was a god. By entering the underworld, he had gained his long-awaited powers. He even defeated the original God in a duel, thereby proving his strength.

But there was still one thing that eluded him —the secret of immortality. As a god, Lucifer instantly became immortal the moment he returned to the underworld. His wife, however, was only a mortal. If she were to stay by his side forever, he'd need her to become immortal. *What if I'm selfish for thinking this way?* he thought. He shook his head. It wasn't completely selfish; Luna wanted to stay with him forever as well. He'd be fulfilling her wishes, as he had always promised to do.

He turned to his left and looked at Luna. She laid on her side, sleeping peacefully. They had a great time an hour ago, and he couldn't wait for her to wake up again. Lucifer gently brushed that strand of her hair that always covered her face, getting a better look at her. *I want her to stay by my side forever,* he thought. *If I am to be happy, to be a good God, I need her by my side. To ensure my strength over Satan, to protect those dear to me... Yes, I must make her immortal.*

—

Satan was drinking wine while Melanie and Risa were fanning him with their giant palm leaves when Lucifer came in. Satan frowned at his son. He didn't like the kid. Didn't want to talk to him at all. The less contact he had with him, the better. After all, he didn't like to not be the most powerful being in the room. Satan sighed and put down his bottle of wine. Exasperated, Satan spoke, "Well... *son...* what is it?"

Lucifer nodded slightly to his stepmothers before speaking.

"Melanie, Risa."

They nodded back to him, acknowledging his presence; which momentarily paused the fanning of Satan, making him even more annoyed.

Lucifer then turned his attention to Satan and said, "Father, I come here today to ask a simple favour."

Satan looked at him, annoyed, as usual.

The chances he's going to help me are pretty slim, thought Lucifer. He continued his request. "I'd like to know how to make a mortal 'immortal'."

Satan appeared frozen for a moment before laughing. "You can't be serious, Lucifer. You're already immortal," he snarled.

Lucifer stood still, unmoving. His face remained serious. Satan narrowed his eyes, realizing what he meant, then said, "You're fucking serious, ain't you. Perhaps—it has to do with the little shark-toothed pussy of yours? Well... I'll tell you when you kill me."

Satan started to laugh hysterically. That was a clear no; because if he was dead he wouldn't be able to talk. This was one way he had power over

Lucifer, and he thoroughly enjoyed it.

While disappointed, Lucifer's face seemed unchanged as he responded. "I expect no less from you, *Satan*. I will find out for myself then. I am a god too, after all. I will find a way."

As he turned and walked away, Satan slapped his knee and cackled after him.

"You sure fucking know me, son. HA HA HA!"

—

Now at the entrance of the castle, Lucifer racked his mind on what to do. He knew that he could do it; he just didn't know how. There was a library in the underworld—maybe it had a book about immortality in it? While he was pondering to himself, a floating Grim crept up, ready to help his lord.

"My lord, I heard you asking about a way for immortality. For your wife, I presume?" asked Grim, calmly.

Lucifer turned and glanced at Grim. Grim

often appeared ominous, and often appeared out of nowhere randomly, but always seemed to help. Lucifer answered, "Yes. As you probably overheard, my father won't relinquish that information to me."

Grim floated around a bit before responding. He said, "I'm not sure if I will get in trouble for this. But I've been around longer than almost anyone here. I know how to do it, but it's better if you learn for yourself. Come, my lord, follow me."

With a gesture from his see-through arm, he beckoned for Lucifer to follow. Curious, Lucifer trailed after Grim's floating figure.

They soon reached the entrance to the library; it was inside the castle, deep into the labyrinth of walls and doors, of which Grim navigated with ease.

At the door, Grim motioned with his hand, as if welcoming Lucifer into the building. Lucifer stepped in and immediately noticed the musty smell.

Grim floated inside and started to light up the candles, one by one. The library was vast, filled with books from shelf to shelf. There was plenty of dust caking up the room, which might've been giving off the smell. There must've been thousands of books there; unless Grim knew which book it was, this was definitely going to take a while.

When Grim finished lighting up the library candles with his ghostly flame, he motioned for Lucifer to follow him again. He led him to the back corner of the room, where a noticeably less dusty bookshelf lay.

"Behind this bookshelf is a secret room. Inside that room are secret books that only a select few may look at; just your father, me, and now you," said Grim. He turned around then seemed to fumble around one of the books. Then, the bookshelf made a clicking noise. "Ah, it's open now," stated Grim.

He pushed the bookshelf backwards and it

opened up. Behind it was indeed a room, albeit a small one. Inside the room was a single ancient bookshelf, decorated with a few books. Nearby was a wood table, a red-painted chair, a candle stand that hung from the short ceiling, and the smell of an unfamiliar type of flower.

"Sometimes I go in here to be alone," said Grim, proudly. "As you can see, there's no dust in here. I keep it very clean."

Lucifer walked into the room, and peered around. The ceiling candle lit the wooden room, casting around it a soft orange-yellow glow. On the table was a book, already opened. Grim hastily moved over to the table, closed the book, then set it back on the shelf.

"That's not the one you're looking for, that's my personal book. Ahem. Anyway... let's see," muttered Grim, as he rummaged through the bookshelf. He hadn't taken out the book of immortality for a long time, and he forgot where he last put it. Finally, he found it. It was a black book with a simple illustration on the cover; the symbol of a snake around a rod. Grim flipped through a few pages before setting the book down on the table. He said, "These two pages are what you need to know. Make sure you follow the instructions carefully. If you need me, I'll be in the library, cleaning up the dust. The library's gotten quite dusty over the millennia."

Lucifer nodded to Grim and sat down on the chair. It was only two pages; the text was quite large, and there were illustrations. It didn't seem too complicated.

Step 1: The immortal shall cut themself and fill up a vial with their blood.
Step 2: The mortal shall drink said vial.
Step 3: The immortal shall stab the mortal in the heart, through their back.
Step 4: The immortal shall collect the mortal's heart blood into another vial.

Step 5: The mortal shall drink said vial.

And... that was it. Step three concerned Lucifer. Wouldn't that kill the mortal before they could drink the heart's blood? He shook his thoughts away. *No, I have to trust Grim. He's already read this and knows it. He just wants me to learn it too.* Lucifer mentally took notes and memorized the steps. *Cut, drink. Stab, drink. That's it... it's easy,* he thought. It shouldn't take any longer than a few minutes to complete. Gathering himself, Lucifer stood up, out of the chair. He closed the book of immortality and placed it back into its place on the shelf. He closed his eyes and breathed out. He was ready.

–

Luna was surprised at first, but didn't hesitate to agree. She trusted Lucifer with all her heart, after all —emotionally and *literally*. They sat on the balcony floor of their castle room. Lucifer had prepared two vials and had a knife to do the cutting. He looked at

Luna, who seemed unafraid of what was to come. She smiled at him and caressed his leg, reassuring him. Her voice was strong, but Lucifer could hear a semblance of fear in it.

"I'm ready whenever you are, darling."

Lucifer held the knife to his arm. He had to do everything very quickly—especially the latter steps. After taking a breath in and then out, he told Luna, "Okay. I'm starting."

Lucifer stabbed his arm lightly, then cut it open, slightly more. Some blood started to pour out. He grabbed the first vial and held it under the wound. In a few seconds, the vial was filled up. He quickly grabbed a tourniquet and wrapped it around his arm, then motioned for Luna. She held the vial to her mouth then poured it down. She gulped down the red liquid; once empty, she gave the vial back to Lucifer.

Luna then turned around—now was the hard part. She would have to take a direct stab to her heart and somehow survive long enough to drink her own blood. Lucifer put his hand on her shoulder, scared to do it. *Mortals can't take a hit to the heart and survive... I'm scared, scared for both of us.*

"Do it quickly, darling. I'll manage myself, like I always have," she said. She gave a big smile to Lucifer; if nothing else, she had to look brave in front of him, to give him confidence.

Lucifer nodded; it was now or never. Still, he couldn't help but to slightly tremble as he thrust the blade into her heart. It went in smoothly, as if her body was nothing. Compared to him, her body was so weak; so fragile.

Luna let out a ghastly cry which faded quickly. She went limp as a veritable mountain of blood poured out of her wound. Lucifer, shaking in panic now, put the next vial under her bleeding heart. It filled up quickly—too quickly. Her blood was leaving her body too fast. Now, with tears in his eyes, he put the vial to Luna's mouth. She was not moving—how could she drink?

He covered up the heart wound with his knee to slow down the bleeding; by doing so, his leg started to drench with her blood. Then, he tilted her motionless head back. He poured the blood from the vial into her mouth until there was not a single drop left.

Luna remained still; motionless. Lucifer cradled her in his arms.

You can't be dead. You promised me.

You promised me!

–

Luna coughed up some blood, which landed on Lucifer's chest. She slowly opened those sparkling green eyes and looked up at Lucifer. His eyes were red and full of tears, evidence of his pain. Luna gave him a small grin and whispered softly, "How many times have I told you, I can manage myself?"

Lucifer cradled her and cried like he had never before. That could not be more true, for he had never cried before. Not when his adoptive parents passed, not when he learned of his birth mother's demise. But perhaps it was everything at once that caused him to cry.

As he sobbed in Luna's embrace, she comforted him.

"There, there. Keep crying and you're going to make me cry, too," she said, in her sweet yet raspy voice.

Lucifer tried to wipe away his tears, but more still came. *This is getting embarrassing,* he thought, *I need to stop crying.*

Luna went in close to him and gave him a kiss. She whispered, "There you go. A kiss to make the tears go away."

With that, Lucifer's tears started to falter, until he was no longer crying. His eyes were red, his nose stuffy. He looked a mess—but that didn't matter, as Luna survived. Luna was now *immortal.*

Grim slowly floated up to the balcony

where Lucifer and Luna were. He'd been watching from afar and finally came to talk after Lucifer stopped crying.

"I didn't tell you this, my Lord, but the mortal will briefly die before they become immortal. I wasn't sure if you'd do it you knew," said Grim.

Lucifer turned around and spotted Grim. So he'd been watching, in the distance, making sure everything went well. Lucifer responded, "Nothing can stop me from what I want to do, Grim." He glanced at Luna, who was beaming at him with her one-of-a-kind dagger-toothed smile. Lucifer continued, "Unless my lady decides otherwise."

Grim bowed his head, preparing to leave.

"I shall now leave you two alone. If you ever need my assistance, I am always here at your command."

With that, Grim slowly floated away from the balcony, leaving the couple alone to enjoy each other's company.

–

"I am a deadly succubus, despised and feared by all. A demon. A monster. A cold, uncaring husk of a being. Now I am immortal… thanks to you, darling," said Luna. She laid on top of Lucifer on their bed together, her athletic body squishing into Lucifer.

She gave him another kiss before continuing. "I still sometimes wonder why this handsome god chose me. Even now, I'd still like to know."

She peered into his face, expecting an answer. He had shown his love for her through his actions, sometimes his words. But he never told her why he accepted her.

"You saved my life multiple times, Luna. Have you forgotten?" said Lucifer. He had fallen for her during the second time they met; even though he didn't show it, he'd been ecstatic with joy when she asked to join him on his journey. She was his support and bodyguard at the same time, a loyal partner

who would always be by his side. She was
everything he wanted and more.

"Oh, and of course, your sexy body doesn't
hurt either," whispered Lucifer. Luna gave him
another kiss, then laid upon his warm torso with her
supple hips, preparing for yet another session. Lucifer's body, which was the most powerful in the
world, at this moment felt so soothing and comforting. Luna could never get used to it, could never not
get excited. It was pure bliss during times like this,
when they simply enjoyed each other's company.
And, with her now being immortal, they could enjoy
life together for eternity.

She remembered all the hard times she'd
faced; her tumultuous youth as an orphan, the countless scores of hunters who tried to kill her. Living
alone in that stone building in the middle of the
forest. Shivering in the cold winters as she went out
to forage for food, to hunt. She had lived a difficult,
stressful life; but now it was different. With Lucifer

by her side, she'd never have to struggle again.

I suffered for so long... but in the end, I made it out. It's because of you, Luc, thought Luna, as she straddled the handsome god in front of her.

I'm in heaven and hell at the same time.

Wonderful, isn't it?

EPILOGUE

———

On planet Earth, there are two gods. One is good, the other evil. Both from the same world, yet molded by different environments. One, the father of all: Satan. The creator and the destroyer. He who gave up on His creations long ago. He lives only for Himself; for indeed, He is all.

—

The other, Lord Lucifer. Son of Satan, he was the one prophesied to slay his father. He who was raised by mortals. He who is kind, compassionate, and has forgiveness in His heart. He who judges by the content of one's character, not the content of one's appearance.

—

There was one, but now there are two. In that sense, humans were partially right. Perhaps it was intuition; perhaps something more...

THE END

Map of Terre

Milky Way • Sol • Earth • Terre

– Characters of Terre –

THE UNDERWORLD

Satan	God, the Devil, Heavenly Father, Holy Father; *maker*
Lucifer	Son of God, General of Terre; *Terror of Khaeru, Terror Knight*
Lumia	First wife of Satan, Lucia's mother
Melanie	Second wife of Satan; *Melly*
Risa	Third wife of Satan
Lucia	Fourth wife of Satan, Lucifer's mother
Grim	The Grim Reaper; *Death*
Paisy	Maid of the underworld
Palo	Vineyard worker who wears all white

– Characters of Terre –

THE KINGDOM OF BASTEA

Luna	A succubus; *She-Devil, Demon Maiden*
Bjol Merscheaunt	A travelling merchant
Renald Bastea	King of Terre
Lenkl Deniere	Lord of Northern Terre, General
Mary Deniere	Wife of Lenkl, mother of Lucifer
Johnny Mackintosh	Friend of Lenkl, Sergeant
Junell Karisman	Leader of coalition forces, Rebel General
Agenwa Karisman	Lord of Zundan, Rebel General
Tehla Tengen	Lord of Yvyerst, Rebel Commander
Ponto Picuno	Rebel soldier

Jack Oth	Bastea courtyard guard, conscripted
John Oth	Kanton gate guard, conscripted
Len Monro	Kanton gate guard, conscripted

– Characters of Terre –
THE KINGDOM OF PSUERT

Vakzi Rakcizs	King of Eastern Terre; *the coward King*
Gronc Grenada	Royal Commander
Tom Whipplesworth	Royal bodyguard
Jiit Geto	Commander of Psuert, under Carn
Carn Eje	Leader of the five master swordsmen of Psuert, under Ranken
Ben Jamen	Second master swordsmen of Psuert
Carl Ington	Third master swordsmen of Psuert
John Nhe	Fourth master swordsmen of Psuert

Feics Nuse	Last master swordsmen of Psuert
Jimmy	Hooded sellsword
Matthew	

– Characters of Terre –

THE DEVIL'S CULT

Sunk Ranken	Dictator–King of Terre
Mizo Creiz	Count of Khaeru; *Vampire*
Segundo Seguno	Commander of Kanton
Weasel Wisle	Commander of Bastea; *The right-hand*
Siig Geto	Lieutenant of Bastea; *South Watch*
Eddie Dreid	Commander of Yvyerst; *Dread*
Jack Jones	Lieutenant of Rottendoom
Behr Gweitt	Lieutenant of Gruppen; *Bear*
Wehr Gweitt	Baron of Gruppen
Zwein Zitosi	Lord of Rottendoom, Ranken's champion
Lang Langanol	Warlord of Northern Terre
Ayr Desmann	Aide to the Gweitts

| Ofh Sanu | Foreman in Gruppen appointed by Wehr |

Author's note

— — — —

It's about what's inside, not outside, that matters

most.

A drawing of Argua from "**9 2 5**"

"Argua spins in excitement."